IN THESE PAGES

A collection of short stories by

Heather Caruso

Illustrated by Tao Caruso

Ordering Information:
For large quantity order email the author at: heathercarusoauthor@gmail.com

Written by Heather Caruso
Illustrated by Tao Caruso
Cover Design by Artistic Warrior

ISBN: 978-1-987982-48-0 (paperback)

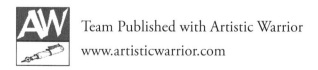

Team Published with Artistic Warrior
www.artisticwarrior.com

In These Pages

This book is dedicated to Tao, my tech support,
who has been a great help with this book.

And to my sisters: Marilyn, Rosalie, and Cassandra.
You have always been there for me with
your never-ending emotional encouragement.

Heather Caruso

In These Pages

Table of Contents

Heather Caruso

In These Pages

Infatuation

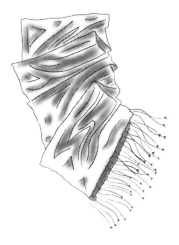

He noticed the mid-thigh black dress and the length of her legs. A mane of red hair framed her face and accented her green eyes. Aaron held his breath and watched as she nibbled on a muffin and glanced around the mall's food court. She caught him staring at her. Their eyes met. Did the floor tremble under his feet?

He knew her name was Samantha by looking at her name tag. She lowered her lashes and scanned the pages of a romance novel. Aaron could make out the title: Infatuation. He felt he had to meet her.

Samantha looked at her watch and stashed her book in her handbag. Her lips lingered on the straw as she took a last slow sip of her drink before she tossed it into the trash on her way to the escalator. Aaron followed.

He was mesmerized at the sway of her hips and the way she walked with ease on red stilettos.

She entered a boutique on the second floor, so he sat on a bench outside the shop and watched as she straightened a display of sweaters. Easy listening music played through the mall speakers. To Aaron, it sounded like angels singing and Samantha's every step was in sync. Oblivious to the shoppers, their chatter, and the smell of popcorn that rose up from the lower floor, he was only interested in her. He wasn't ready to approach or speak to her yet. He was worried she might notice him, so he left.

When Aaron was in class, or at the library trying to concentrate on Grade 12 math, he dreamed about Samantha's soft plump lips covering his, and how her pale skin would feel to the touch. He blushed at his own thoughts. On the pages of his calculus book, letters and numbers transformed into her face.

Aaron, almost seventeen, had never had a girlfriend. His fourteen-year-old brother had a girlfriend and girls called him all the time. He teased Aaron about not liking girls, but in fact, Aaron thought the girls his age were silly, and giggled too much. Samantha, however, was a different story.

After his Friday afternoon classes, Aaron headed to the mall again. Before going to the boutique, he checked himself out in a shop window. His slim frame and shaggy black hair made him look younger than his age. He wondered if, maybe, he should have gotten a haircut. Was his white T-shirt with Led Zeppelin on the front the right thing to wear? Was it cool?

As he stood outside the boutique, his stomach pulsated like a beehive. With both hands in the pockets of his jeans, his shoulders up to his ears, he watched her.

He pretended to be interested in the window display. When he glanced up, she motioned with her head for him to enter. He took a deep breath and stepped through the door.

"Hey," she said.

"Hey," he replied.

"Are you looking for a gift for someone?" Her sweet, smooth voice did little to relax him. He could hear and feel his heart pounding as loud as the drums in a rock band.

Aaron glanced around the shop at all the women's clothing and glitzy jewelry. He rested one hand on the showcase to steady himself.

"It's my mom's birthday," he blurted.

"Oh, how nice. Have you thought about what she would like?"

He didn't answer as his mind raced. It wasn't even his mother's birthday. He felt heat rising from his neck to his cheeks. He looked down at his feet and hoped she wouldn't see his crimson face.

"Maybe I can suggest something," Samantha said as she reached into the glass showcase that separated them. "We just got in some lovely silk scarves."

Aaron shifted his feet and nodded.

A blonde girl came out of the dressing room with a purple dress over her arm and stood behind him.

Samantha set three brightly coloured scarves on the counter. She picked up the turquoise one. The blonde girl took a step closer to Aaron to examine the scarves. He could feel her breath on his neck. She smelled like mint and flowers.

"This is very nice," Samantha said as she stroked the fabric. "What do you think?"

"Some lucky girl will be happy with that gift," the blonde interjected.

Aaron felt trapped. He glanced over his shoulder and checked to see how far he was from the door.

"I'll take it," he said.

"Would you like it gift-wrapped?" Samantha held up silver wrapping paper.

"Gift-wrapped? Oh, gift-wrapped. Sure."

As Samantha wrapped the gift, Aaron focused on the silver chain that rested in the rise of her breasts.

"There you go," she said as she placed the present in front of him and primped the turquoise bow.

He looked at her perfect hands and broke into a sweat. Samantha was wearing a wedding ring.

"Your mom will love this scarf," she said. "With tax, that will be two hundred and sixty-nine dollars. Will that be cash or credit?"

Aaron stood still like a frightened rabbit. He patted his pockets and looked up at his never-to-be girlfriend. "I'll be right back," he said as he dashed out of the store. He took the escalator steps two at a time, hoping she wasn't watching. He ran through the mall and out into the parking lot. By the time he reached the street where he lived, he was exhausted. He stopped for a moment and rested on a bench at the bus stop.

"Are you okay?" a female asked.

Aaron looked up to see the most beautiful girl in the world.

"Yeah," he said. He took in a couple of deep breaths and exhaled slowly. She had such pretty eyes and a great smile. "My name is Aaron." He smiled back at her, his infatuation with the redhead almost forgotten.

Not In Service

Jean stood on the front step of her son's three-bedroom bungalow and savoured each puff of her cigarette.

Brad appeared at the door. "Mom, the smoke's coming through the screen. Hillary's upset. The baby, you know."

"Sorry, Brad," Jean said, and she moved to the sidewalk. She leaned against a tree trunk to support her aching back. She'd suffered from chronic back pain ever since she slipped on icy stairs a few years ago and damaged a disc. The cigarette hung from her lip as she closed her sweater against the spring wind.

When the cigarette was finished, she crushed the butt on the sidewalk with the toe of her running shoe. She wondered if she should go back inside or go for a walk. A screeching sound came from above. She looked up and saw several crows. Jean shuddered. Crows were synonymous with death. She went inside.

In her small room, door closed, she felt like a chastised teen. There was no headboard for the single bed that was flush against the wall. She sat on her pillow at the head of the bed and leaned back. She sighed deeply, pulled her knees towards her chest and covered herself with a patchwork quilt. There was nothing in the room that made it her own except the few things in the top dresser drawer. In that drawer were several decks of cards, bingo dabbers, and four packs of cigarettes. A silver box held a tiny pair of white baby shoes tied together with the laces. They were Brad's first pair of shoes, with his name printed on the sole. There was a Polaroid picture of Jean with Brad's dad as she held Brad in her arms.

Jean thought about Josh, Brad's father. A grey cloud of guilt washed over her. Five years ago, Josh had died suddenly from a rare heart condition. He left her with the house and a bank account. Josh's death and the casino coming to town were simultaneous. It took her less than two years to gamble it all away.

She looked up and noticed, for the first time, tiny sparkling stars on the ceiling. They reminded her of the childhood room she'd shared with her sister, Carrie. It had had the same sparkling stars.

Jean got up, grabbed a deck of cards and sat back on the bed. The slight breeze and the shuffling sounds the cards made gave her the feeling of a place she loved to be:

the casino. She shifted to a more comfortable position. Her back was really bothering her tonight. There was no pain medication this month because her cheque had been left at the casino.

She was startled when her daughter-in-law knocked on the bedroom door. "Jean," she called. Jean jumped off the bed and cards flew everywhere. "Are you in there? I'm going outside to water the plants. Zack will be awake soon. Will you watch him?"

Jean took a deep breath and opened the door. "Sure, where is he?"

"In his crib." Hillary waved her hand in front of her face. "Jean, can you please change that sweater? You smell like smoke."

She quickly gathered up the cards, put them away, and changed her sweater. She opened the dresser drawer, took out Brad's baby shoes, and put them in her sweater pocket. She headed down to Zack's room and watched him as he slept in his baby-blue sleepers. She could hardly believe how beautiful he was. She placed her hands over her heart. He looked so much like his dad.

She wished she had been a better mother to Brad, her only child. Many evenings she had chosen to go to bingo and left Brad and his dad at home. One night, Brad had hung on to her leg. "Mommy, I want you to read my story tonight. Please, Mommy." She was torn, but the call to the

Bingo Palace won.

Zack woke and Jean picked him up and carried him to the change table. She changed his diaper, dressed him, and carried him to the living room. She took him over to the window and saw Hillary outside with a broom.

Jean watched as Hillary swept the one cigarette butt off the sidewalk, shaking her head.

Jean looked at Zack and said, "I won't do that again."

Hillary was the quintessential housewife. Brad had learned quickly there was a place and time for everything. Jean suspected their sex life was scheduled in, like everything else. Every second Saturday was marked on the calendar in the shape of a heart.

Jean put Zack in his highchair and kissed his little sock feet. She took Brad's baby shoes out of her pocket and put them on his feet. A perfect fit. "You are so handsome," she said. "Just like your daddy."

Hillary came into the kitchen, looked at the shoes, and smiled. "You've kept Brad's baby shoes all these years?"

Jean nodded.

"I did something right," she whispered to Zack.

She had been living with Brad and Hillary for a couple of months now. She was grateful they took her in when she was on the verge of homelessness, but she knew she had to watch every step. Never leave a cardigan on the back of a chair. Never leave a cup in the sink. And for goodness' sake, never leave cigarette butts around.

She was a middle-aged woman living with her son and uptight daughter-in-law. She wondered if this was what the rest of her life would be like. She realized, with disheartened clarity, that it could very well be if she didn't help herself.

Jean was forty-nine. She was still pretty and a bit too thin, with a hint of grey woven through her ash-blond hair. The tiny dice earrings that dangled from her earlobes were a permanent part of her look.

Brad had suggested she join a seniors' club, or maybe an online dating service. She had told him in no uncertain terms that she was not a senior yet. As for dating, there was no way she would do that. What if she met an axe murderer?

What Jean really wanted to say to him was: Who would want her? Who would take that risk? What did she have to bring to a relationship? Nothing. Nothing at all.

Jean wondered if Brad shared anecdotes with Hillary about growing up with a mother who had addictions. She thought about the time she had to choose between a toy Brad wanted and a pack of cigarettes. She bought the cigarettes while he cried.

A few days later, as Zack slept, the two women sat at the kitchen table preparing potatoes and green beans. Jean, who rarely initiated conversation with her daughter-in-law, searched for something to say. "I won a hundred dollars at the casino last night," she said, and immediately realized it was the wrong thing to say.

Hillary got up and went to the sink to wash the beans. She grabbed a pot from the cupboard, filled it with cold water and plunked it down on the stove. She turned to face Jean, arms folded as she leaned against the counter. Jean braced herself.

"So, you haven't had yourself banned from the casino yet?"

Jean was caught off guard and dropped the potato peeler on the floor.

"No, but I plan to." She picked up the peeler.

Hillary lifted her chin and rolled her eyes in unveiled skepticism.

"Do you know what I was thinking, though?" Jean said as she stood and brought the peeled potatoes to the counter. "I saw an ad today. They want people to work at the casino. It pays well and they train you to work at the card tables. I can already shuffle like the best of them. Want to see? I'll show you." Jean looked at Hillary's open mouth. Another mistake.

"Jean, that's ridiculous."

Jean left the kitchen and headed towards her room. Hillary followed her down the hall with her hands on her hips. "A gambler like you, working at the casino? For

God's sake, Jean. What are you thinking? You told us you would quit gambling when we took you in. Why not get a job at the mall?"

Jean felt trapped. Hillary was too close. She felt crushed by her presence. She stepped into the bathroom and left Hillary standing in the hall. She restrained herself from slamming the door shut. Her anxiety brought on a hot flash and sweat dripped from her forehead into her eyes.

In the mirror she noticed how nicotine was taking a toll on her skin. She bent over the sink, filled her palms with cold water and splashed her face several times, hoping to wash away the evidence of her destructive life.

She took a perfectly arranged towel from the rack and dried her face and hands. She left it scrunched up on the vanity. When she came out, Hillary wasn't there.

Jean went to her room and sat on her bed. She didn't bother to shuffle cards.

What Hillary didn't know was that Jean had already answered two ads for clerks at the mall. They wanted young women with high heels, short skirts, and cleavage. At least, that's what the twenty-something girls looked like who had interviewed her. In one of the interviews, she'd had a coughing attack. Her smoker's cough always happened at the worst times. She knew not to expect a call.

On Monday morning, Jean went to the casino to have herself banned. She was doing it for Brad. She entered an office where a blonde woman with big hair and a ring on every finger sat behind a desk. She motioned to a chair. Jean sat down.

"Well, Jean. What brings you to my office?"

As if she didn't know, Jean thought.

The woman extended her hand. "I'm Marion."

Jean took her hand. "How do you know my name?"

"I work here, Jean. I'm here every day. I know the regulars." She tapped a pen a few times on her desk as if to say, "Let's get this done".

"I'm here to have myself banned." Jean's voice was a whisper.

Marion pulled out a sheet of paper from her desk drawer and went over the form. She explained how it worked. Face recognition at the door and a signature. That was all it took. She passed Jean a pen.

Jean took the pen in her limp hand but didn't have the strength to sign.

"Are you ready to do this?"

Jean's tongue was fat and dry, and she couldn't speak. Her clothes were wet. The room became the size of a small closet. Whatever smidgen of courage Jean had was swallowed up by Marion's heavy musk perfume. Her heart raced at the thought of abandoning her only friend.

She stood and ran out of the office. The pen fell silently on the red and blue carpet.

***

The atmosphere at the casino embraced Jean. The sounds of the machines were like musical notes cheering her on to fulfill a dream of the big win. Being with like-minded people, who didn't judge each other, made her feel at home.

Every month she promised to at least limit herself. Jean knew her addictions were corroding her soul. She thought of herself as a super-loser. Her energy was zapped and her will, well, there was none. She tried taking only twenty dollars to the casino, but when the twenty was gone, her inner voice teased her. *This is the night, Jean. It's time for a big win. Just a few more times should do it.*

But after several trips to the bank machine, the voice was proven wrong. Her monthly check was gone in one evening. It would be twenty-eight days before the next one. She knew how upset Brad would be. He'd find out because she'd have to ask him for cigarette money. She ran out of the casino and headed for home.

After dinner, Jean needed a cigarette. She found Brad in the garage as he leaned under the hood of his car.

"Brad, honey, I ran short." She coughed and leaned

down to look at the engine as if she was interested. "How people are expected to survive on a pittance, I'll never know."

"Mom. Again?" Brad straightened up and let out a big sigh. He brushed his sandy hair off his forehead and motioned for Jean to move. Then he slammed the hood shut. "You promised to quit smoking and to quit going to the casino, Mom. When will you do that? When it's too late? Have you seen a doctor about that cough?"

She never told him that she had seen the doctor. He'd told her she had COPD. He'd given her a few sample puffers. "It will help with your breathing," he'd said. "And if you quit smoking, it may prolong your life."

She knew Brad would end up giving her money after the usual sermon. Then she saw Hillary peering into the garage from the kitchen door. She leaned against the doorframe, arms folded, ankles crossed, with a tight smile on her face.

"Now, Jean, you know we won't be helping by enabling your problem. No money this time, Jean." She looked to her husband for backup. He nodded in agreement and Hillary left.

"What's with this destructive nature of yours, Mom?" Brad asked as he threw a screwdriver in the toolbox. It landed with a clang. His voice was louder than normal. "You need help, Mom. Can't you see it?"

He closed the toolbox and walked over to her. His voice softened. "Mom, I know someone." He took a business card from his wallet and passed it to Jean. "Will you see her? She's a psychologist who specializes in addictions. A guy at work had great success after seeing her."

Jean took the card. She wanted to ask if he talked about his poor old mother and her addictions to the people at work. But she knew he cared, and let it go.

She looked at the card and then at the wallet still in Brad's hand. She glanced up and noticed Hillary was back in the doorway giving Brad a warning look. He put the wallet back in his pocket. Hillary went back into the house.

Brad hated being between his mother and his wife. But no matter what, Jean was still his mother. He put his arm around her shoulders as if to protect her. "You can do it, Mom. Start by cutting back on smoking. Limit yourself at the casino and see this doctor." He tapped the card. "I'll pay for it."

She looked up at him and patted his cheek.

***

That night Jean dreamed she was a teenager again. She could hear her mother's voice echoing in her dream.

"Jean, why are you smoking?"

"Jean, your teacher phoned today."

"Jean, why can't you be like your sister?"

Jean woke from her restless sleep. She thought about the last time she saw her sister, Carrie, many years ago. They were standing on the lawn arguing. Carrie was begging Jean to go to a party with her. Jean told her she had other plans. She didn't. Being with her younger, smarter, prettier sister made her feel inferior to the point where she wanted to hide.

Jean wished with all her might she could delete the memory of the night two police officers came to their door in the middle of the night. And the soul-wrenching sound her mother made when they told her Carrie was dead.

Jean got up and went into the kitchen to make tea. After all these years she still wondered if Carrie would be alive today if she had gone with her that night. Would she have gotten into that car with a drunk driver? Would she too have been killed?

All Jean knew was that her mother never recovered. For the next couple of years, she could feel her mother's eyes following her around the house. Her head didn't move, only her eyes. Jean knew her mother wished it had been her, not Carrie, who died that night. Jean often wished it had been her who died that night.

The next day, Jean washed the lunch dishes and watched Hillary in the garden from the kitchen window.

It was a pretty picture: the young mother in a bright pink tank top and jeans. Her blond hair glistened in the sun. She held a bouquet of tulips and smiled as she showed them to her baby.

As Jean finished the dishes and wiped the table, she saw Hillary's purse sitting on the chair, wide open with a fat wallet inside. Before she knew what she was doing, she had a ten-dollar bill in her hand. A little less than the price of a pack of cigarettes. She had a couple of dollars in change in her purse to make up the difference. She would replace the money for sure when she got her next cheque.

She was putting the wallet back in the purse when Hillary walked in.

"Jean!" Hillary yelled. "Really? Stealing from me! What have you reduced yourself to? A thief? Now I can't even leave you alone in my house." She glared at Jean. "I'm calling Brad," she said. She grabbed the bill from Jean's hand, tucked her purse securely under one arm and stomped from the kitchen with Zack in her other arm. The tulips lay spread out across the table.

Jean stood there white-faced, her mouth open, but nothing came out. The kitchen was silent except for the sound of the ticking clock.

Jean knew there was nothing she could say to Hillary to defend herself. She wanted to say, "I am not a thief. I've never stolen anything in my life. I would've paid you back."

It had happened so fast she barely remembered making the conscious decision to do it. Should she deny it to Brad? No, she couldn't lie and put more stress on him.

If there had been time for a second thought, would she have put the money back if Hillary hadn't caught her? She didn't know. She needed a cigarette.

Jean walked around the block once, twice, three times. The pain in her back was fierce now, but she couldn't go back inside. Could she ever go back inside?

Jean thought about Hillary's comment that she could not be left alone in the house. She wondered if she was really a thief if she planned on giving it back. She decided the answer was yes.

Jean had had her lows. She had collected butts from public ashtrays, lipstick and all. But stealing from the people who had taken her in was the worst. She'd reached the darkest corner of her life.

As Jean paced up and down the street in front of the house, she saw Hillary in the living room window, watching her. Jean reached into her back pocket and felt her bus pass. It was Thursday, the day the casino served free coffee. Someone there would loan her a cigarette.

She had missed the bus by a few minutes. It would be another twenty minutes before the next one.

Large clouds rolled in and blotted out the sun. Within minutes it was raining, and Jean was soaked. She stood alone at the bus stop wearing only a T-shirt and capris, with pain radiating from her lower back. She winced and grasped the pole for support. The heavy rain bounced off the pavement as cars sped past, splashing water up onto the sidewalk and soaking her to the bone. This was her punishment. This was the price she had to pay for her sins.

Jean stood on the sidewalk, consumed with misery and guilt. The rain felt like tiny hammers beating on her shoulders. It stung her face and she closed her eyes. Brad's disappointed face appeared before her. She could never look him in the eyes again.

Something dark and ugly from her core taunted her. Her own voice echoed in her head: "You're a thief, a lost cause, a burden. It should have been you, not Carrie."

She looked up to see a bus speeding towards her with its *Not in Service* sign flashing.

Jean stepped off the curb.

That Thing

In a small town outside of Rome, a man took a batch of small, colourful good-luck elves out of the kiln. He placed them on a metal rack to cool. They all had the same mischievous grin, and all had red hats. Twelve, plus one, were made at a time. There was always an extra in case one was flawed. If one was not perfect, it was to be broken and thrown away.

The thirteenth in this batch had a bright green jacket. The man looked closely and noticed a small scratch down the left side from its eye to its toe. He was about to destroy it when he remembered he hadn't had time to pick up a gift for his daughter's birthday. When no one was looking, he dropped the pint-sized elf into his pocket.

At home, his daughter ran to him. She jumped up and

down, excited to see her gift. He handed her the elf.

Her smile disappeared. "What's this, Papa?"

"It's a good-luck elf. Buon compleanno, my daughter."

The girl walked away, disappointed and without a thank-you. Outside, she put it down on the street and kicked it along, like a stone. After a few blocks she smiled, thinking about the cake and ice cream she knew her father would have for her. She kicked the elf into a ditch. She was going to have a happy birthday.

Later that day, two boys happened along. They found the elf and played catch with it. Back and forth. Back and forth. Up in the air, down in the dirt. When they were bored, they threw the elf in back the ditch. They laughed and raced each other back to their homes.

Carlo was the next person to find the elf. He had a table at a flea market in Rome. He was always on the lookout for odd things to sell. He put one foot in the ditch, picked up the elf, and said out loud, "Where did this dense-looking thing come from?" He turned it over in his hand and shrugged. "But I guess it's kind of cute." He plunged the elf deep into his pocket. He decided to sell it as a good-luck charm. "Some mindless dummy will buy you," he said.

When he tried to pull his right foot out of the ditch, his left foot slid down and twisted at an odd angle. "Owwww!" he screamed. The pain was intense. He tried to stand on it to see if it was broken or just sprained. He was able to stand, but barely. He pulled himself out of the ditch and limped along the road. He decided to take a shortcut through a field. He needed to get home and put some ice on his ankle.

If only he hadn't picked that thing up. He limped along and muttered to himself, "What did I do to deserve this? All I did was pick up a stupid inanimate object."

The words had barely left his mouth when he slipped into a pile of dog poop and fell on his bottom.

The next day he sold the cursed thing to the first person who gave him an offer.

***

Christopher paced around his house and tried to shake off a sense of foreboding. He'd felt that way since he'd returned from Rome with the grinning elf statue.

Today he felt weak and weary. He pushed his black-rimmed glasses back up his nose and rubbed his hands together to stop them from shaking. He opened the back door, took a deep breath of fresh air, then went back inside to the living room.

As he looked out the window, he felt a sense of relief when he saw his friend Luke pull into the driveway. They greeted each other at the front door and thumped each other on their backs. Christopher closed the door and guided Luke into the kitchen.

"Can I make you some fresh coffee?" Christopher asked.

"To hell with coffee. I could use a beer," Luke said.

"Oh, of course, what was I thinking?" Christopher slapped the side of his head. He opened the fridge and grabbed two beers. He passed one to Luke, who twisted the cap off and took a big swig.

"It's about time you came back home. How's Toronto?" Christopher asked.

"Busy. Too busy for me. I'm glad to be home. I missed Jenny and the kids. A month was too long to be away from them."

They chatted about the Toronto traffic, and about the business Luke had to deal with there. Then something caught Luke's eye. A weird little elf with pointed ears and piercing eyes sat on a kitchen shelf, a smirk on its face. "What the hell is that?"

"It's an elf. What does it look like, an elephant?"

"I could hardly mistake a silly elf for a freaking elephant." Luke went over to the shelf and picked up the elf. He held it between two fingers and waved it in the air. "Creepy little thing, isn't it? Look at that evil face."

"Hey, for Christ's sake, be careful with that. Give it to me."

Luke passed it to Christopher, who blew on it to remove any possible dust, then placed it back on the shelf.

"What's with you? Why are you making a fuss over a stupid ornament?"

Christopher squinted his eyes and gritted his teeth. He grabbed Luke by the arm and practically dragged him outside to the cedar-fringed patio.

"Listen, Luke," he said as he pushed his glasses higher on his nose. His face was pale, and his voice cracked. "You can't say things like that in there. I know this sounds crazy, but that thing has evil powers, or something. My house feels dark, even when the sun shines. It . . . it's making me nervous and uncomfortable in my own home. One night I slept in my car." He ran his hands through his dark hair.

Christopher told Luke about Anna, his cleaning lady. She had told him the elf had grinned and winked at her when she was dusting it. He didn't know if he was horrified or relieved—relieved that someone else had witnessed the sinister antics of the stupid thing, or horrified that he had confirmation. Anna had called a few days later and given her notice.

Luke broke in. "Maybe it was just the sun shining in her eyes through the blinds. How did you end up with that dumb thing anyway?" He folded his arms and lowered his chin, ready to listen.

Christopher gestured towards the patio table.

"Sit down," he said.

Luke sat and Christopher sat across from him. "Well, you know the trip I took this spring to Italy?"

"Yeah, you mean you got that thing there? That's an odd souvenir to bring back from Italy."

Christopher thought back to how his life had come to this: being afraid of an ornament. About two years ago he had won a dinner for two at the Grand Hotel. Since then, he had entered every contest he came across. He bought tickets for cars, houses, and trips. The two-week trip to Italy was his biggest prize.

He took a gulp of beer and began his account of how he acquired the elf.

"It was when I was visiting Rome. The weather was perfect, a balmy twenty-six degrees," he said as he took a sip of his beer. "I was standing in line with my tour group at the Sistine Chapel. We were told there was a two-hour wait because of the lineup of tourists. I wasn't that interested in the chapel anyway, so I decided to explore the streets, mingle with the locals and take in the sights and sounds."

Luke nodded. "Go on."

"Well, I came across a large white tent on a side street outside the Vatican. There were tables full of souvenirs. Not the usual artwork, rosaries and statues. There were games, scarves and colourful dishes. I made my way through the crowd and stopped at this table full of odds and ends. Ashtrays, Italian flags, fridge magnets, boomerangs, and one tiny elf. The vendor saw me pick it up and came over to talk to me. He told me it was good luck. He said it would bring me good luck if I was good to it. Before I could answer, he'd wrapped it in paper and told me it was only two euro. That's about three bucks Canadian, so I bought it."

"So why are you afraid of a trinket that's supposed to bring you good luck?" Luke asked.

"Well, it was weird," Christopher continued. "As I left, I saw the man wipe the back of his hand across his forehead, and he gave a sigh of what sounded like relief. I wondered how long he had been trying to sell the elf."

"So, what's the big deal? And what do you mean by evil powers?"

"Well, if you let me finish, I'll tell you."

Luke shrugged.

"When I got home and unpacked, I put the box away in the garage and forgot about it. I came across it recently. When I opened it, I saw the elf's left arm was broken right off and it had a scratch starting at its left eye and all down its left side. I threw it and its arm in the trash bin in the garage. It was only three bucks, no big loss there."

"But it's on the shelf now." Luke said.

"Yeah," Christopher said. "The next morning, as I was

about to get into my car, I decided to shake out the mats. I pulled one out and I fell backwards, flat on my back, and couldn't get up because my left arm hurt like hell. The doctor said it was broken, and I had a cast put on it."

"Your point?"

"Don't you get it? It was my left arm. Same as the elf."

Luke laughed. When his last chortle died down, he noticed Christopher's pale face. He composed his own features into a semblance of empathy, patted Christopher on the back, and spoke in a comforting tone. "Haven't you ever heard of coincidences, old buddy? A coincidence, that's all it was."

"Think what you like, Luke, but there's more." Christopher finished off his beer in a single gulp. "I had a freaking rash all down my left side, from my eye, and under my cast and down my leg to my little toe. The doctor said he had never seen anything like it."

"What's wrong with your doctor? Even I could tell you it was probably an allergy to the cast material."

"You didn't see it, Luke. It was weird. It had red bumps, and each bump was circled by green dots. Well, anyway, that's not all. The next day I woke up with a swollen eye."

"I suppose it was your left eye," Luke said. He pursed his lips as if to clamp the laughter that wanted to escape.

"Yes! It was my left eye," Christopher said as he jabbed the air near his eye. "That's my point, all my ailments were on my left side. Like the elf's left arm and that scratch down its side. I feel like I'm being punished for throwing it and its arm in the trash."

Christopher looked at his empty beer, stood, and started to walk away. He'd hoped Luke would be more sympathetic. He needed to talk to someone about the elf.

Luke sensed his gloominess, got up and put a hand on Christopher's arm. "Wait, Christopher," he said. "I'm sorry I upset you, but what the hell? You have to admit this sounds strange. Sit back down and talk. Let's have another beer."

"Yeah, I'll get it." Christopher walked towards the kitchen door as he massaged his left temple.

Luke waited. He was torn between mystification and amusement.

Christopher returned from the kitchen with an opened bottle of beer in each hand and gave one to Luke. He remained standing and set his beer on the table. He undid the top three buttons of his shirt. The patio was hot in the afternoon sun. He gripped the back of his chair, his head hanging down.

"Come on, sit down." Luke patted the chair.

Christopher sat and took a gulp of beer. He leaned forward and looked directly at his friend. "I want to tell you the rest, if you'll just listen."

"Okay, I promise to listen," Luke said.

"I came home from a follow-up doctor's appointment. He said my arm was taking its time to heal. Anyway, when I got back home, I went into the garage and passed by the trash bin. That thing was on the floor beside it. It was sprinkled with coffee grounds. Don't ask me how it got there. I know I had thrown it into the bin. As I said, that thing has powers. It looked at me with that evil expression. I picked it up and decided to wash and repair it. I thought I'd better be safe rather than sorry and treat it well, for my own sake. Christopher paused. "You know, when I was in Rome, that vendor told me that if I was good to it, I'd have good luck." He took another swig of beer and continued his tale. "I dumped out the trash, found the arm and glued it back on. Then I got out some paint and touched it up. Then I placed it on the shelf in the kitchen where you saw it. And guess what? The next day, my rash disappeared, my eye got better, and my arm started to heal."

"Holy shit, you don't really believe that thing caused your broken arm, a rash, and a swollen eye, do you?" Luke was beginning to doubt his friend's sanity.

"It was all on the left side," Christopher interjected.

"And," Luke continued, "because you fixed it and placed it on a shelf in the kitchen, you got better?"

"Yes, I believe that's true," Christopher said. Then he leaned over the table and whispered, "To tell you the truth, I would like to get rid of it. Or, should I say, find it a good home. But I'm scared to. I'm worried I'll make a mistake and suffer the consequences."

"Oh, come on, Christopher. What's wrong with you? It's just a hunk of clay or plaster or whatever." Luke moved to the same side of the table, closer to his friend. "I go to Toronto, I come back to see my friend, and I find someone I don't think I know. We've been friends for years now. I didn't know you were this superstitious."

"I know, I know, I can't help it." Christopher put his beer on the table. "I don't know what to do." He leaned forward, put both elbows on the table and buried his face in his hands. The pair sat there in silence. After a moment, Christopher stood and started to walk in circles. Luke followed him.

"I'll tell you what," Luke said. "How about I take it off your hands?"

Christopher stopped walking. "What will you do with it?"

"Hell, I don't know. I'll take it home. It won't be your responsibility anymore. So you can relax."

Christopher put both hands on Luke's shoulders. "Are you sure, Luke?" He spoke in a low voice. "I told you it's evil. You'll have to take care of it, for your own sake. I don't want anything to happen to you."

"For Christ's sake, I'll be fine. Your worries are over, old buddy."

As Luke left, he laughed to himself and placed the elf on the dash. He wondered what in the world had gotten into his friend. He'd always thought Christopher to be a fairly sensible guy.

Clouds had gathered and become heavy with rain. Within seconds they let loose and a river of water ran through the streets.

Luke stopped at a red light and looked at the elf. "You sure are creepy-looking," he said. The elf appeared to be glaring at him. "Well, good luck to you, creep," Luke said. "I hope you can swim." He pulled over to the curb, rolled down the passenger window, leaned over and tossed the elf into the gutter. He watched as it was carried away towards the storm drain.

Luke was about two kilometers from home when his windows fogged up. Then his wipers stopped, and the defogger wouldn't work.

"Holy shit," he yelled and gripped the steering wheel as he approached the old wooden bridge. The tires took over as if they had a mind of their own. His brake pedal was loose. He panicked and tried to undo his seatbelt. It seized up. He lost control of the car, skidded through the wooden railing, and landed in the river.

He remembered what Christopher had said. "Take care of it, for your own sake."

The water was halfway up his windows and seeping

through the vents. He couldn't open the door. He looked around for something to smash the window with, but there was nothing.

I'm going to die here, he thought as the faces of his wife and kids flashed before him.

Just then, the car's fogged windows magically cleared, and he was able to undo his seatbelt. He held his breath and clicked on the window switch. It opened. Water gushed into the car. Luke held his breath and squeezed through the window.

He was a strong swimmer and made it through the rushing water. As he sat on the riverbank trying to get his breath, he saw the elf perched on the roof of the car. Was it warning him?

"Shit . . . shit . . . shit," he muttered.

He swam back through the water to the elf. He snatched it in his fist and made it back to the riverbank. He put it in the breast pocket of his shirt and walked the rest of the way home. The rain finally stopped, and the only sound was the sloshing of his water-filled shoes. He patted his pocket a few times to make sure the elf was safe.

Now in his own kitchen, Luke took the elf from his pocket and placed it on a shelf. His wife, Lora, appeared. "Did you get caught in that downpour? You're soaking wet." She kissed his cheek. Over his shoulder she saw the elf. She picked it up, held it between two fingers, and waved it in the air. "Where did this silly thing come from? Look at that evil grin."

Luke's face turned white. He grabbed the elf, put it back on the shelf, and hugged his wife. "Let's just keep it safe. I was told if you treat it right, you'll have good luck."

She shrugged. "Whatever you say, honey."

The Garden Visit

I didn't listen to Grandma when she told me to never go into the garden at night. I told her I wouldn't, but I asked her why. She wouldn't tell me, and that made me want to go all the more.

So, I, a girl as curious as a cat, went to the garden that night. I sat under the kiwi-covered arbor on a not-very-comfortable rustic bench and waited. I didn't know what I was waiting for. I saw the lights in the house turn off one by one as everyone went to bed. There was no moon, so I couldn't see my hands in front of my face. I listened to the shiny leaves of the kiwi vines playing in the breeze. The scent of lavender wafted over from another part of the garden. It was so relaxing out here.

"Gina!" my grandma yelled.

I screamed and the lights went on in the house, casting enough light for me to see my grandmother in front of me. She folded her arms over her long black robe. A few strands of silver hair sprung out from their usual order.

"Didn't I tell you not to come out here at night?"

My heart pounded. I'd been caught. "I'm sorry, Grandma. I won't do it again," I said as I ran back into the house.

The next morning, we all sat at the kitchen table for breakfast. Me, my parents, my little brother, and Grandma. I watched Grandma's face. She didn't look at me. She sipped tea from her Old Country Roses china cup and saucer. She avoided my inquisitive stare. If she thought I would let this mystery go, she was mistaken.

She wasn't like other grandmas her age who dressed in pastel stretch pants and flowered blouses. No, she had long platinum hair in a ponytail. She wore long skirts and black turtleneck T-shirts adorned with colourful scarves. I admired the three long silver chains she wore around her neck. Their sparkle fascinated me, as did their meaning. One was a string of tiny hearts. The second was a mixture of hearts and keys, and the third was a string of small oval discs with the letters R and S engraved on every one. Regina and Simon.

My mom told me the chains were gifts from Grandpa. He gave her one for her wedding gift. The second and third he had given to her for their twenty-fifth and fiftieth wedding anniversaries. Mom said Grandma had worn them every day since Grandpa passed away.

And Grandma had false eyelashes. She didn't have them when she came to live with us. One day she went shopping and came home sporting them. I said to my mom, "First I see eyelashes coming around the corner, then I see Grandma behind them."

Mom tried to suppress a giggle and whispered, "Stop that!"

Grandma's name was Regina, but Grandpa called her Gina, and sometimes, Peaches. I was named after her. We should have had a better relationship, but I couldn't relate to her—or, I should say, we couldn't relate to each other. She wasn't like my friends' grandmas, who showered them with kisses and hugs when they came to visit. I was okay with that.

Grandma had been living with us for two months. She was my father's mother. She and Grandpa had lived in a small town on Cape Breton Island. After Grandpa died, Dad insisted she come to live with us in the Okanagan. The thing she liked most about living with us was the prolific garden that consisted of a mixture of flowers, vegetables, and fruit and nut trees.

I knew she was watching me, so I resisted the urge to investigate the garden at night again. Grandma and I had an unspoken contest to see who could stay awake the longest. She won every time.

It looked like I would never get a chance to spend time out there, to satisfy my curiosity and to see if Grandma frequented the garden herself at night. But a few weeks later, I got my chance. Grandma went to bed early, so I told Mom and Dad I was going to my room to do my homework.

I did homework to pass the time until it was dark. I tiptoed by Grandma's room and listened at the door. I heard soft snoring. She was asleep. Now was my chance.

I met my little brother Billy in the hall, wearing his Spider-Man pajamas. "Go to bed, you little creep," I said.

The screen door at the back of the house had a squeak if you opened it too far. I inched it open just enough to squeeze out. I sat on the bench and waited. I focused on the white Shasta daisies that glowed in the light of the full moon.

I heard the squeak of the screen door and saw Grandma coming towards the garden. I ducked behind a large box of potting soil and sat cross-legged on some mulch between a stack of plastic pots and a shovel. Grandma sat on the bench.

A half-hour passed. I was getting sore and the mulch was itchy. I wondered how I could sneak away.

Then I heard voices. It was Grandma talking to Grandpa. I recognized his strong, yet soft voice. But he was dead. How could this be? I peeked over the box, but

I couldn't see him. It was obvious Grandma could, as she sat with her body turned to the side and looked up as if she was looking into his face.

"You're late," she said.

"Sorry, Peaches. I had errands to do."

"Simon, you're dead. What kind of errands would you have to do?"

"Oh, there's lots to do here. I can't move on just yet."

"Simon, you're losing me. Aren't you in Heaven?"

"No, I'm on the outskirts of Heaven; but Gina, I had a glimpse. It's so hard to describe."

My body tensed and I shivered. Was I actually listening to my dead grandfather about to describe Heaven?

"For mercy's sake, Simon, try," she said. "You were never at a loss for words before. Tell me what you saw."

"And you were never patient, Peaches." I heard my grandpa's distinct laugh. "Okay, I'll try. Just after I passed, I was standing outside the gate. It was huge and not made of pearls. It had the look of black wrought iron, but it glistened. It was energy and it seemed like I could have put my hand through it. A woman and a little girl, holding hands, passed by me. The gates opened for them. I tried to follow, but I was stopped by a force I couldn't see. What I saw and heard is beyond description."

"Why didn't you tell me this before?" Grandma asked. "It's been over two months. You should have told me."

"I didn't want to worry you," Grandpa said. "But I'm okay, and I know I'll get in soon."

Grandma shifted on the bench and said, "Can you describe what you saw?"

"I'll try. There was soft melodic music, but it felt powerful. It embraced me with love."

"Really?" Grandma said as she put her hands to her face. "And what did you see?"

"Like I said, I had only a glimpse. There was light inside. Light that was so soft. It looked like it was made of trillions of moving specks. I saw beings floating in the air. They were a concentration of the light. I mean, there was light and there were thicker versions of it. I think they were angels."

Grandma folded her hands and held them to her heart. "Did they have wings?"

"No, but they were wearing robes in colours I had never seen before. Impossible to describe. It would be like trying to describe the taste of an orange to someone who has never tasted an orange before."

I was so taken with the conversation. I wanted to stand and ask Grandpa to tell me more about the colours, but I was afraid he would leave. I shifted for comfort and knocked over the shovel. I think Grandma was so engaged in Grandpa's description of Heaven that she didn't notice the soft sound when it landed on the mulch.

"Go on, Simon. What else? Tell me. Tell me."

"Well, as I said, I wasn't in Heaven, but it was amazing. I was told what to do. There was no language, just a knowing, and I followed that knowing. I was told to come be with you. There's something I have to tell you, Peaches. You'll be joining me soon."

I felt my heart pound faster. No, not Grandma, too. We didn't get along that well, but I did love her and didn't want her to go. I leaned in and listened more intently.

"I'll be joining you soon? When, Simon? When?" Grandma sounded happy.

"You have three months to prepare. That's all I can say."

"Oh my gosh." Grandma stood and danced like a kid who had just gotten her dream gift.

"Sit down beside me," he said softly. So, she sat. One of her hands was raised, as if he were holding it.

"How are our beautiful grandchildren?" he asked.

"Gina's fine. She's almost a teenager. She gives Billy a hard time, though."

I almost said something, but held it in.

Grandpa laughed. "That will pass. But there is one thing I would like you to do."

"What is it, Simon?"

"I would like you to connect with our granddaughter."

My eyes opened wide and I almost spoke. Grandma

was quiet for a moment, as if she didn't understand. Grandpa waited as he took her hand again. Then she nodded. "I can do that," she said in a soft voice. "What about you, Simon? Will you be ready for me when I cross over?"

"Yes. It's much easier over here. I'll be ready."

"You said you have errands to do. What are they?"

I leaned closer. What on earth could my dead grandpa be doing if he wasn't in Heaven?

"I was appointed to help people who are scared to cross over. I have a list. When that's done, I'll be ready to enter Heaven with you."

"Are you coming back again?" Grandma asked. "I miss you so much."

"No," he said. "But I'll be waiting for you so we can go through the gates of Heaven together."

Grandma stood, and it looked like she was getting a hug.

"Oh, and Peaches," Grandpa said. "What's with the eyelashes?"

"I like them," she said. "Don't you?"

"I like them," he said. "Such a pretty woman you are."

When he left, I felt a warmth go past me. Then I felt someone tousle my hair. Goosebumps ran up and down my spine. I waited for Grandma to go into the house and then quietly snuck into my room.

I really wanted to tell my mother that Grandpa had been in the garden, but I felt like I should be the keeper of a secret.

Grandma changed after the garden visit. Well, I guess we both changed. I was nicer to Billy and I tried to get closer to Grandma.

One day I offered to make her tea. She said only if I would have some with her. We sat face to face at the kitchen table. Grandma sipped from her china cup and I drank from my mug. She asked me questions about school and if there was a boy I liked.

She came to one of my basketball games with my parents. When the game was over, she told me she had been on a basketball team in high school. We did a high-five. She told me that whenever she saw a game on TV, she remembered the excitement in the air and the smell of the gym.

The next day after breakfast, I found Grandma sitting in a straight-backed chair by the front window. Her legs were crossed, and her long skirt was draped over them. I asked her to play basketball with me. "Grandma, let's go out in the driveway and try a few baskets."

She looked at me as if I'd asked her to fly to the moon.

"Come on, Grandma, we'll take turns."

She smiled and said, "Oh no. Not me."

"Just a few tries. It'll be fun," I said.

It didn't take too much persuading before she was up and following me outside.

I went first and missed. I tried again and the ball dropped right into the basket. Grandma clapped her hands and smiled at me.

"Your turn, Grandma." She stepped up and I handed her the ball. She bounced it a few times. She concentrated on the basket before throwing the ball. She missed. We both giggled.

Grandma never did make a basket that day, but the smiles and giggles from the two of us made a memory for me. I had never seen her laugh before. After that day, Grandma and I grew closer and I came to enjoy the time we spent together.

Three months after Grandpa's garden visit, Grandma passed over. My mom told me to wake her for breakfast. I went into her room and knew by the stillness that something was different. I bent over and looked closely at her on the bed. Her eyes were closed, and she was smiling. I knew then she was gone.

I rushed into the kitchen. Mom was placing a platter of pancakes on the table. Dad was laughing as he arm-wrestled with Billy. I looked at Grandma's cup and saucer and wondered what we would do with it. In a hushed tone I said, "Grandma's dead." Dad dashed down the hall into her room. Mom put her hands on my shoulders and whispered, "Help Billy get ready and take him to school."

Why we were whispering, I didn't know. But the moment had a sacred quality to it. Mom kissed my forehead and gave me a gentle push.

On the way out the door, I picked up my backpack. In the side mesh pocket, I saw something sparkle. I pulled out Grandma's three silver chains. I held them to my heart as they hung between my fingers. I took Billy's hand and cried on the way to school.

"Are you crying because Grandma died?" he asked.

We stopped walking and I looked into his innocent face. "No, these are happy tears. Grandma is in Heaven. We'll miss her."

He nodded in agreement.

After Grandma's passing, I had so many questions. I spent many nights in the garden, wearing her silver chains as I hoped she would visit.

I'm still waiting.

Zeena's Story

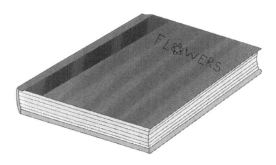

Why Anna had the sudden urge to write this story was a mystery to her. Her children were grown and lived on the west coast. She lived on the east coast and rarely saw them. Her husband, Bill, spent his days in his workshop building canoes. Anna's life was about her books, her garden, and her dog. Never had she written a story—until now.

It started with a series of dreams she had three nights in a row. Every detail of the dreams was as clear as if they had actually happened. Even though she was standing in her kitchen, staring at the open dishwasher, she was actually somewhere between the kitchen and her dreams. She shook her head, loaded the dishwasher, and then walked her dog.

When she came back, the dreams were still with her. She decided to sit at her computer and write. It was strange how the story came to her. There was no advance warning, just the flow of dialogue and narration. She went with it.

Zeena was a fifteen-year-old girl. Her parents were born in Africa, while she was born into slavery on a plantation. She was an inquisitive child who asked questions that most girls her age and circumstance never thought about.

Her grandmother, Gama, as Zeena called her, was willing to give her the time she needed, and did the best she could to answer all of her questions.

"Why can't we have books, Gama?" Zeena asked as she watched her grandmother scrub a blue shirt on a washboard. "I saw books in the big house. Lots of them. They said I wasn't to touch them. But I did." She tilted her head, stuffed her hands into her apron pockets, and waited for her grandmother's response.

"Please stay out of trouble, child," Gama said. "Be a good girl and help me with the laundry." She patted Zeena's cheek with a soapy hand and passed her a bag of pegs.

"But I want to know what's in them, Gama. What's in those books? What do they say? I saw a really nice one with pictures of dogs, and one with flowers. They were so pretty." She held the bag of pegs and handed them to her grandmother one by one.

When the laundry was all hung on the line, her grandmother bent down and looked directly into Zeena's face. "The world is in those books, Zeena. Everything you ever want to know." She straightened up with her hands on the small of her back. "But that isn't for us." She pulled Zeena closer and lowered her voice to a whisper. "Although, I feel in my bones, the day will come. If not for you, for your children. The day will come, girl. We will be free. We will have choices."

"And books?" Zeena asked.

"Yes, child, and books."

Leroy McMaster, the plantation owner, felt it was his right to have his way with any woman or girl he fancied. His slaves were his property.

Zeena walked behind a row of cabins, where she was less visible and enjoyed the yellow and gold wildflowers mixed with lavender. She twirled in the new red skirt her mother had made for her.

Leroy happened to be coming down the path. For the first time, he noticed how beautiful Zeena had become.

He asked her where she was going as he adjusted his broad-brimmed hat and leaned against a tree.

"I'm going to finish my work in the house," she said, and quickened her step.

Leroy lunged and grabbed her arm.

"Forget that for now," he demanded. "You come with me." He tightened his grip and led her away.

Zeena knew her time had come. Leroy's evil grin was a giveaway. Her mother had told her to stay clear of him. Leroy had taken her mother far too many times. She remembered the look on her mother's face when Leroy came for her. She felt her father's silent rage because he was powerless to stop it. Zeena had made up her mind a long time ago that Leroy would never take her as he had her mother. She had planned to avoid him and never look him in the eye. But now, it was too late.

Zeena was unprepared for what happened. Her slender body didn't stand a chance against this forceful man. She cried herself to sleep that night and many nights after. She dreamed of ways to kill him. There were many ways, and they were all long and torturous. She wanted to see pain in his face as he was reduced to tears and begged for mercy. Her hate for Leroy consumed her.

***

Anna pushed away from the computer. She felt for Zeena as if she had experienced the horrible act herself.

That night, she couldn't sleep. Instead she lay there silently weeping for the girl in her story. In the middle of the night she got up and took a shower.

The next morning, she described Leroy to her husband and told him of her dream and her obsession with writing Zeena's story.

Bill told her it was just a dream, and to find another

interest. Then he asked her if she'd fixed his work pants yet. Before she could answer, he stood, drank the last mouthful of coffee, and went out to his workshop.

It wasn't long before Zeena knew she was going to have a baby. She didn't want Leroy's child and she knew he wouldn't want it either. He'd never claimed any of the children he fathered with his slaves.

Her parents watched as their once gentle daughter became temperamental and consumed with anger. She threw pots and pans and refused to help her grandmother.

When the time came for the baby to be born, they called the midwife.

"Come on Zeena, scream," the woman said. "It helps. They all do it. Scream, Zeena."

Zeena did not scream. She held the bedpost in a death grip and breathed heavily. The long painful labour was almost too much for such a young girl.

Finally, Zeena gave birth to a baby boy. He had curly black hair and large wide-set eyes like his mother. The baby had Leroy's green eyes.

When the baby was placed on Zeena's chest, she would not look at him. She pushed him away and rolled over to face the wall.

The midwife said, "Zeena, you have a beautiful baby boy. Look at him." Zeena pretended not to hear. She chanted a childhood poem and refused the child.

Zeena's family took care of the baby, hoping Zeena would at least name him. "Call him what you want. I don't care," she said as she sat on the veranda in a rocker, her arms folded.

Her family came up with a plan. They would leave Zeena alone with the baby. Her mother would not be far.

The baby soon woke up and began to cry. Zeena ignored him. He cried louder. She ran around and kicked everything in her path. She called for someone to tend to him. No one came. When she couldn't stand his crying any longer, she summoned the courage to peek into the cradle. He stopped crying and looked up at her.

Zeena was amazed at what she saw. She didn't see Leroy's child, nor a child born from a violent act. She saw a trusting little soul dependent on her. She picked him up and fed him the bottle her mother had conveniently left on the table.

Zeena named him, Obi. The name meant "joy."

When Zeena was out with Obi and Leroy was around, she covered the baby's face. She wouldn't allow Leroy to lay eyes on the child, not if she could help it. She was never without rocks tucked in her pockets.

Leroy left her alone. Maybe he saw her fill her pockets with rocks. Maybe he felt her strong hate for him. Or maybe she wasn't what he wanted any more. After all, there were other girls.

Zeena made promises to her baby. To protect him forever and, above all, to see that he learned to read and write. She'd heard of a woman on another plantation who taught children to read. She would find a way.

***

Anna stopped typing. She was delighted with the bond of mother and child. She cried with happiness. She had done her best to tell Zeena's story and was satisfied, though she still didn't understand why she had felt the urgency to do so.

With Anna's dreams about Zeena on paper, she felt her job was done. She sometimes wondered why the dreams had been so real. She wondered why she felt she'd actually been there, on the plantation, watching it all happen. She printed out the story, put it in her desk, and left it there.

Anna's life returned to normal. After a time, she felt comfortable enough to share her story with friends. On the first Tuesday of every month, she met Jennifer and Mary at Spencer's Café. They had lunch and a discussion about the book they'd agreed to read the month before. As they were chatting about the book they'd recently read, Anna related the story of her dreams of Zeena and how she felt so close to the girl.

Her friends listened intently without interruption as

Anna described Zeena's life. Jennifer didn't have input or suggestions as to why Anna had had this experience. But Mary did.

"Maybe you were having a past life experience. You know, maybe you were Zeena in another life and the memory came back to you in dreams."

Anna sat there with her mouth open. She knew little about past lives. Could this be her answer?

The three ladies continued to chat about anything and everything and then, like always, they walked over to the bookstore. Anna found a book on canoe-building that she was sure Bill would love. Jennifer found a book on yoga.

Anna continued to look through the books, hoping to find one she could get into. Then Mary rushed over to Anna with a book in her hand. "You have to read this," she said.

Anna took it from her: *Proof of Past Lives*. Maybe there was an answer out there after all.

Brenda Brandon

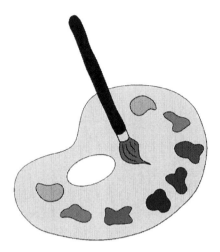

We all knew that Brenda Brandon was going to Hell because Mother St. Mary said so. She stood in front of the seven-year-old girl and waved her finger.

"You'll burn in the fires of Hell, Brenda Brandon," the nun said as she nodded in the affirmative. "You're always late, your homework is never done, and your deportment . . . well, I'll have to speak to your mother!"

Brenda appeared to accept the authoritative prophecy. She sat there, one hand under her chin and looked straight ahead, but not at the nun.

I imagined Brenda rolling in flames like a side of beef, forever in her brown plaid cotton dress, the only thing she ever wore.

As Mother St. Mary promised, Brenda's mother was called to the school. As my vision of Brenda rolling in the flames of Hell stayed with me, so did that of her mother.

The classroom door opened. A fancy woman in high heels stepped in. Her hair was piled on top of her head in dramatic fashion. Red lipstick pronounced her lips. Her diamond earrings sparkled. The mink stole over a tight green dress gave her the look of a movie star.

Whispers swept through the class. "You know who that is?" one girl asked. "It's Brenda's mother."

Another girl added, "My mom says she's crazy."

I remember going home that day and describing Mrs. Brandon to my mom.

"Poor, Brenda," Mom said, then she gave me a hug.

I was particularly curious about Brenda and decided to be her friend. I couldn't play with her at recess because she had to stay in because her homework wasn't done. I waited until school was over. Then, on the way home, I caught up to her and walked beside her.

"Hi," I said. She didn't reply, so we walked in silence. I noticed how small she was and found it easy to keep up with her quick little steps. Her brown dress had a yellow stain on the front. Mustard, I guessed. After a few blocks of walking in silence, she turned down a side street. I didn't follow, but I hollered, "Bye!" She didn't answer.

She was outside at recess the next day.

"Wanna play with us?" I asked. Us being my friend April and I.

Brenda looked at us suspiciously. "Why?" she asked. Then she looked down and kicked at the gravel.

"We're going to play catch," I said.

She stood there and I thought she was going to say yes. Instead she said that she would watch, and she did.

April was quite the comedian. She made faces, exaggerated her ball catching skills, and was just being silly. Brenda never smiled at any of her antics. Even when April missed the ball and did a silly dance all the way over to the fence to retrieve it, Brenda's face was blank.

A few weeks went by. I walked home from school with Brenda every day. Mostly she was uncommunicative. I concentrated on the cracks in the sidewalk and hopped over them.

One day she surprised me. "Bye!" she said as she hopped over a crack before she turned the corner. I decided to follow her. I watched as she entered the gate of a white two-story Victorian house with a wrap-around veranda and hanging baskets of red geraniums. It looked like my dream house.

A few weeks more went by and Brenda started talking to me. Not a lot, and she didn't volunteer much personal information. One time she said, "My mother doesn't like me most of the time." I didn't know what to say to that.

In the mornings she started waiting for me on the corner. One day she smiled and waved when she saw me.

"Julie, Julie," she called. I barely recognized her. The brown dress was gone. She was wearing a pretty pink dress. With her curly brown hair and big brown eyes, the pink looked great on her.

"My Auntie Jo is here," she said. "She brought me this dress." Brenda was grinning from ear to hear. She looked great, all clean, no stains, and her hair was done up with a white ribbon. She still wore her old brown shoes.

At school that morning, Mother St. Mary asked us to display our homework on our desks. I cringed as Brenda pulled out hers. Mother St. Mary tucked her arms up the sleeves of her habit and walked up and down the aisles, glancing down at the notebooks. When she got to Brenda's, she picked it up.

"Good work, Brenda," she said and continued on. I thought I saw the nun smile.

***

The end of the school year arrived, and Brenda squeaked by to Grade 3. Her aunt outfitted her with the clothes and shoes she would need for the summer. We spent our vacation together and Brenda, April and I became good friends. All summer we romped and played.

One day, my mother suggested we all take an art class. April and I were excited, but Brenda wasn't sure. We had to coax her into it. The next day she told us her aunt had signed her up. We'd all be going to art classes that summer.

We loved the weekly class and I created some pretty good stuff. April did, too. However, it turned out that Brenda was talented beyond her years. She received constant praise from the teacher, and everyone could see why. She was really good.

When the art classes were almost over, they planned an art show. A few days later my mom got a call that they'd changed the date of the show. The woman asked Mom if she had Brenda's phone number, as it wasn't in the registration forms. I told Mom I didn't know her number, but I'd be happy to go to her house and tell her. I was delighted when Mom agreed that I should go to Brenda's house and let her know the art show date had changed. At last, an excuse to see the inside of her home.

There was no one outside as I climbed the steps to the veranda of the Victorian mansion. As I paused to admire the huge pots of red and white flowers, I heard screaming from inside. I turned to run, but before I could, Brenda's mother burst through the screen door and clamped my wrist. Her brown hair was short now and stood on end. Her eyes were like fire, and all she wore was a full slip.

"I know you're the devil!" she screamed as she tightened her grip. "You can't have my girl! No, you can't have her, she's mine."

The blood drained from my face as her grasp held me tight. A little bit of pee trickled down my legs. Brenda and her aunt dashed outside.

Auntie Jo took the woman's hand and calmly said, "Becky, the tea is ready and I made biscuits."

"Biscuits!" Brenda's mom said in a child-like voice. She let go of my wrist and was guided inside.

Brenda burst into tears. I didn't know what to do. I wanted to run to the safety of my home and to change my underwear. Instead I sat on the porch steps with my arm around Brenda as I tried not to look over my shoulder at the door.

***

As children grow, they learn new things about life. That summer I learned that not every child felt protected at home like April and me. And things were always changing.

On the Labour Day weekend, Brenda came to my house early in the morning. She rarely came over uninvited, so I knew she had something important to say. She was skipping up the sidewalk, so I ran outside to meet her, the screen door slamming behind me. She looked so happy.

When I reached her, she took my hands in hers. "I'm moving to Toronto," she blurted and then stood there will a big grin on her face.

"What?" I couldn't believe she'd be moving.

"My Aunty Jo is going home and she's taking me with her. She bought me a new suitcase. It's my favourite colour, blue."

I was speechless. Brenda was leaving me.

She threw her arms around my neck. "I'll miss you so much. But I promise I'll write every day."

She let go of me and before I could say anything, Brenda ran down the street. She stopped and turned. "Say bye to April for me."

***

I don't know what happened to Brenda's mother. The house was eventually sold and there was a rumour that she was placed in an asylum. My mom said that Brenda's mom was sick and needed help, so they sent her to a psychiatric hospital.

Brenda never mentioned her father, ever, so I didn't know where he was. Our town was small and of course there was no shortage of rumours. One of them was that a wealthy man from the States, who never married Brenda's mother, had been supporting them.

I waited every day for a month, but I never got a letter from Brenda. After a few months, I realized she was never going to write to me. I'd lost my friend.

Twenty years passed and one day I received an invitation to the opening of an art show in Toronto. It was a one-woman show featuring a new artist: Brenda Brandon. There was a hand-written note at the bottom.

This might never have happened if you hadn't been my friend and talked me into those art classes many summers ago. The evening would be perfect if you would attend as my special guest. We have so much to catch up on!

Yours truly,
Brenda

You're a Big Girl Now

At breakfast, my mother said, "Megan, you know that guy at work I told you about, the really cute one? Well, he's asked me out for drinks and dinner after work. I'm excited." She had a wide smile as she sat down at the kitchen table to do her nails. "You're a big girl now. You'll be okay. When I was your age, I had my first job at the corner store. I've been earning money for myself, and then for the two of us, ever since." She waved her left hand in the air to dry her nails and held a mug of coffee in the other.

"Yes, Mom, you've told me that, many times."

"Don't use that tone with me, Megan. Now off you go. The bus will be here any minute. I'll keep in touch with you, though. And there's mac and cheese in the fridge from last night. All you have to do is stick it in the microwave for two minutes."

The smell of nail polish and polish remover turned me off breakfast. I wrapped my Danish in a serviette and tucked it in my backpack.

"Go on, now. I hear the bus coming. I'll call you after work."

Mom had me when she was sixteen. We lived with her mom, my grandmother. When she was eighteen, we moved out. She managed to support us with a live-in housekeeping job. Nana looked after me in the evenings while Mom took computer courses.

Mom is good to me, but she's busy with her work and her social life. And like she said, I'm a big girl now. I'm twelve. I can take care of myself. But Mom telling me that I'm a big girl now did not inspire confidence in me.

After school, the bus let me off at the end of my driveway. The flag on the mailbox was up. I collected the mail and a gust of wind grabbed one of the flyers. I had to run up the driveway to catch it. I let myself in.

I grabbed a bag of chips and a can of Coke, my usual after-school snack, and settled down to watch TV. A weather warning crawled across the top of the screen. It warned of a severe cold front moving in with heavy snow and high wind.

"Yeah, yeah," I said out loud and changed the

channel to my show.

The snow started falling and the old farmhouse got cold. I hated this house. It was too big for us and some rooms were closed off. The drapes were dusty. The old oak floorboards in the living room were smothered with an ancient rose-patterned rug. The whole house smelled musty. It was as if the house had surrendered to its fate of old age.

Mom promised we would move back to the city when she got her finances in order. This was her brother's farmhouse, and we could live there for free until she'd saved up enough to move back to my friends and my old school.

I got up and looked out the window. I couldn't see the field on the other side of the road. I closed the drapes, sat down again, and pulled a blanket over myself. The wind howled and got on my nerves. I hoped Mom wouldn't be too late. She hadn't called like she said she would.

Mom didn't like me calling her when she was on a date, so I resisted the urge.

I turned the TV back to the local channel.

A storm had blown in from the north. The weatherman warned against going outside without preparation. The sub-zero temperature would freeze exposed skin in seconds.

I went back to my show and turned the sound up to

drown out the wind. It sounded like a banshee howling. We have wind here on the prairie, but the wind that night was epic.

I learned about banshees from my nana. She was a great storyteller. Her thick frizzy red hair was streaked with grey. She didn't care to tame it and it did its own wild thing. When she told stories, her green eyes got bigger and she took on whichever character she was depicting. Some of her ghost stories made me cling to my mother, especially the one about the banshee. I wished she had never told us that one.

Nana was from Scotland and strange stories were a part of life there. The banshee story was about a lost woman's spirit who came to you and howled just before someone close to you was about to die. When Nana realized I was frightened, she tried to reassure me by insisting the banshee was only in Scotland, not in Canada. But I've been scared of howling sounds ever since. Especially a wind like this one.

I broke down and called Mom on her cell. I told her about the storm, and she said not to worry, she would be home soon. Her friend must have been close by because she used her sweet voice. But I knew her. "Soon" could mean anything.

The banshee howl continued, and I held my hands over my ears to muffle the sound. I could still hear it and it sounded just like Nana's description. It started as a low growl and inflated to a high painful shrill that lasted forever.

I phoned Mom again. She didn't pick up. I texted her. No reply. I don't know what was more frightening, the thought that the banshee was a warning about me, or that something terrible would happen to Mom that night. I shook with cold and dread. My teeth chattered and my legs trembled. I called her again and got the "unavailable" recording. I texted her again. No reply. That man from work was much more important than me, I thought. I threw my cell phone across the room. It hit the coffee table leg and came apart.

I went to the kitchen for a drink. Did I see a face in the window over the sink? I put my hands to my face and screamed. If we had neighbours, they would have heard me. Under my breath I said, "You stupid shit-face." I wasn't allowed to use swear words, but I used them when I needed to.

I picked up the house phone. It was dead. I was alone.

The lights flickered and darkness prevailed. The furnace gave up. Where was the flashlight? I remembered it was under the kitchen sink, felt around and found it. I couldn't decide if I should turn it on to see or if I was safer in the dark where I couldn't be seen.

The backscreen door rattled, and I knew it was the

banshee. I would be safer in the dark.

Fear grabbed me in its clutches. I dashed to my room. Hide. I needed to hide. I gathered every quilt and blanket and sat on the floor in the darkest corner. I kept my eyes wide open. I held the flashlight to my chest.

After spending a while shivering in the dark with my arms wrapped around myself, I thought about Nana and the banshee story. Something she said came to me in a flash. She said if a person was brave enough to stand up to the banshee, no one would die. What did that mean, to stand up to the banshee? Did it mean not being scared? Could I do that to save Mom? Yes, I could. I would. I loved her.

I carefully made my way to the front of the house with the flashlight lighting the way. I unlocked the doors and threw open the drapes and curtains as I whistled a happy tune, pretending to be brave. My heart drummed.

When I opened the back door and shone the flashlight into the night, all I saw was blowing snow, but I knew the banshee was watching me.

I danced, sang, and laughed out loud. I waved a dish towel around, pretending to be a matador. I made faces at the kitchen window. After half an hour of these antics, I was almost too tired to be scared.

By six the next morning, the power had clicked on and the furnace kicked in. The wind had calmed, and morning light peaked on the horizon.

Mom had not come home.

I looked out the front window again, watching and waiting for signs of life. Was I the only person in the world? Tears flooded my eyes.

Around eight o'clock, I saw a snow plow on our road. A car followed. It was Mom!

She turned into the long driveway with speed as she tried to get through the snowdrift. She didn't make it. I watched as she left the car and made her way through the snow in her short skirt and high-heeled boots. She had on my jean jacket.

I opened the door to welcome her.

"Hi. How's my girl?" she said as she came in. She looked tired.

"You're alive," I said and threw my arms around her.

"Of course, I'm alive." She patted me on the back. "I couldn't get you on the phone last night and I had to wait for the snow plow this morning. That was quite the storm. Were you okay?"

I told her about the banshee and how I laughed and danced in the face of danger to save her life.

She didn't wait for me to finish. Instead, she interrupted me and said, "I'm beat." She took off my jacket and sat on the chair by the door. She unzipped her knee-high boots and said, "It's chilly in here."

"Mom, I'll make you tea."

"Thanks, honey. And will you throw a couple pieces of bread in the toaster?"

"Okay."

"That's my big girl."

What Happened to Mary-Lee

I asked her to stop. I demanded she stop. I begged her not to see him again. But she just wouldn't listen, so she ended up trapped by evil.

First, I'll tell you a little about Mary-Lee, my fiancée. She was a raven-haired beauty who stood six-foot-one, one inch taller than me. She loved kids, volunteered at the animal shelter, and bought coffee, socks and mitts for the homeless. It was her last year at UBC and we were to be married that summer.

She was adopted, the only child of Lisa and Trevor Gold. They adored her. The only thing she knew about her biological family was that her parents and brother had died in a car accident. She was told she was thrown free and survived because her parents had forgotten to buckle her in. She was only seven-years old.

It all started one day when Mary-Lee tripped and fell while getting off the bus. A stranger caught her. She literally fell into his arms. He helped her pick up her laptop, books and papers, which were strewn all over the sidewalk.

"You need to catch your breath," he said. They walked together for a bit and then he invited her to have a coffee with him.

That evening, she came home to our apartment and told me about the encounter while she chopped lettuce and tomatoes in the kitchen. She suggested we take him to dinner to thank him.

"Anyone who rescued my love is worthy of my attention," I teased. "Okay, we'll take him to dinner. Nowhere expensive, though."

She ran across the room and threw her arms around my neck. I could have lived on her outbursts of affection.

Mary-Lee made the dinner arrangements at a mainstream restaurant. When we arrived, Jayson—that was his name—was already sitting at the table. He stood to greet us.

I have to say, from the handshake on, I was uncomfortable. His cold black eyes made me shiver when he fixed them on me. He was a close talker, and I felt like he was invading my space. I wondered if his intent was to intimidate me. His six-foot-six frame towered over me.

He talked with his hands. Not unusual, right? Except he moved them in sync with his low, smooth voice. One felt the urge to sway or lean as he directed. He enjoyed this power. I could see a hint of amusement in his dark eyes. I resisted the urge to sway. I had to show him I was strong. Meanwhile, Mary-Lee only saw his charming façade.

When we sat down, I couldn't get a word in edgewise. I thanked him for rescuing my fiancée. I stressed that word.

At home, after dinner, while Mary-Lee was vigorously brushing her teeth, I told her how I felt. "I don't like him, Mary-Lee. He never took his eyes off of you the whole evening. He's rude."

"But I like him, Allan," she said.

I snapped my towel in the air. "He ordered extra-rare beef, blue potatoes, and beets. The whole plate was swimming in blood. And you, a vegetarian, ordered the same. What's with that?"

"I don't know," she said. "It was out of my mouth before I knew it." I watched as she put on her black silk pajamas. "It was good, though."

I expected that to be the end of him. It wasn't. We ran into him several times, and it was obvious to me that it was too many times to be accidental. Once at a café, he and Mary-Lee ended up sitting on one side of the table, chairs close together. It was odd—eerie, even—how they looked together. At the same time, it pained me to say, they complemented each other. People stopped to stare at them.

As time passed, Mary-Lee stopped talking about our upcoming wedding. She started skipping classes at school. I didn't know where she was most of the time. When I asked, she accused me of being controlling and suspicious. Suspicious? Maybe. Controlling? Not me.

I asked her outright if she was having an affair. She told me she wasn't, and that she loved me and only me.

That didn't make me feel any better. I was puzzled. The whole thing was a puzzle.

When Jayson called her at home, my suspicions grew stronger. It was weird, because he didn't ask for Mary-Lee. He asked for Veronica.

"There's no Veronica here," I said.

Mary-Lee jumped off the coach and grabbed the phone. "Hi, Jayson. Yes, okay, I'll be there."

I asked what the hell was going on.

"I'll be right back," she said. "I'll explain when I get back!"

And just like that, she was gone.

Unbeknownst to her, I was in hot pursuit. She ran down the main street, winding herself between people. She attempted to cross the street in the middle of the block. I heard the screeching of brakes and yelling and swearing from the man in the truck who had almost hit her. I watched as she made it to the other side, to join him.

Jayson grabbed her hand and was saying something to her. She saw me and her other arm stretched out towards me.

I screamed, "Mary-Lee! Mary-Lee!" A bus intercepted my attempt to cross. When it passed, they were gone.

I didn't hear from her after that. Neither did her broken-hearted mother. Her father had passed away the year before. The police gave up after several months. It would have been a major help if I had known Jayson's last name.

A year passed and I got on with my life. I worked hard to build my accounting business. Finally, I reached a point where I only thought about her once a day.

I was looking for something on top of the closet when an envelope fell onto the floor. I picked it up and opened it. Inside was an old photograph of two black-haired children. I turned it over. "Veronica and Jayson" was written on the back in what looked like a woman's handwriting. The hair on the back of my neck prickled and I ran to the phone.

"Mrs. Gold, I must see you."

"Allan, so nice to hear from you. Is everything okay? Why don't you come over tomorrow afternoon?"

"I'm coming now, Mrs. Gold. I'll be there in twenty minutes." I hung up.

Mrs. Gold led me into her formal living room. A tea tray was set on the coffee table.

I tossed the picture onto the table. "What's this?" I asked.

She picked it up and studied it. "I've never seen this before."

"Come on, Mrs. Gold. You know something."

She stood up and walked behind the sofa, putting her two hands on the back as if to steady herself. "I'm sorry, Allan. You know how much we loved her. She was our only child."

"Mrs. Gold, I don't want to be rude. But get on with it."

"Mary-Lee had a brother," she said.

"Yes, I know. He died in the car accident."

"That's what we told Mary-Lee," she said.

I got up, took her hand and led her back around to the front of the sofa. "Mrs. Gold, sit down, please. Start from the beginning."

She hesitated, sat, folded her hands in her lap and looked me in the eyes. "I want you to know I've never seen that picture before, but the adoption agency did show us a picture of him. This is Mary-Lee and Jayson, her twin brother. Her given name was Veronica, you know. She was such a sweet and happy child. We thought Mary-Lee suited her much better."

"Wait, wait, wait. What are you saying?" I was stunned. I stared at her for a few seconds. "Why didn't you tell the police that Jayson was her twin?" My voice shook.

"Because we never told Mary-Lee about him. We thought she might try to find more information when she was older, so we told her he died with their parents. We were trying to protect her from the stigma of having mental illness in her family. The truth is, the parents were on their way to a home for disturbed children. Jayson was to be evaluated, which meant they had to leave him there." She looked off in the distance. "It was a dreadful crash, the accident."

"So, you're telling me Jayson didn't die? And what's this about mental illness?"

"No, he didn't die. He and Mary-Lee survived. The parents died." She sat back on the sofa and let out a deep sigh. "I'm going to tell you what I've never told another soul," she said. "Not even Mary-Lee."

I braced myself, not knowing what to expect.

"The children were taken to the hospital for minor injuries." Mrs. Gold shook her head sadly. "Once they were deemed healthy enough to be discharged, they took Jayson for a psychiatric evaluation. His medical records showed a history of violence." Mrs. Gold stopped and took a deep breath. "You see, Allan, Jayson was diagnosed with early-onset child psychosis. Schizophrenia, to be exact. They thought he could be dangerous to himself and others. The children's only relative was a young uncle who wasn't in any position to take responsibility for them. He signed off on Mary-Lee's adoption and on Jayson being committed."

I took a deep breath. This was just too much to take in. Mary-Lee had a dangerous brother, who wasn't dead, and she had gone away with him.

"We didn't want a baby," Mrs. Gold continued. "We wanted a girl between the ages of four and seven. Mary-Lee was perfect. The agency told us about Jayson, just in case Mary-Lee asked about her biological family when she grew up. They told us that Jayson always asked about his sister. We were afraid he'd be let out and one day he would find her."

Mrs. Gold stopped and reached for her tea. I sat there, stunned.

She took a sip and put the cup down. "I was selfish," she said. "I really thought she would come back. I didn't think there was any need to tell the police about her brother. As time went on, it got harder and harder to say something."

I pounded my fist on the table. Tea splashed out of the cups. Mrs. Gold's lips quivered. Tears trickled out of her eyes and down her cheeks.

I wasn't proud of myself for making her cry. I could

see how guilty she felt and how much she feared for her daughter.

I took her hand. "Mrs. Gold, I did everything I could to save her. Everything. I begged her not to see him because I knew he was bad news. When she refused, I said that I would go with her so we could both be friends with him. I wanted to protect her. She said no."

"I believe you, Allan. I ask myself every day, 'What happened to Mary-Lee?' Do you think she'll come back some day?"

I didn't respond, because I didn't have an answer. I quietly stood and left without saying goodbye.

I gave the new information to the police. They said they would look into it, but Mary-Lee was an adult, and maybe she didn't want to be found. I protested. They said they would keep the file open and showed me the door.

Ten years have passed now, and still not a word from Mary-Lee. I'm married now, with one child—a girl—and another on the way. I still keep in touch with Mrs. Gold, or Lisa, as I call her now.

What happened to Mary-Lee is still a mystery. And what Jayson said to her on the phone to make her run to him is an even bigger mystery. I don't know why she never tried to get in touch with us. I sometimes wonder if she fell under the spell of an evil man and if, even today, she's trying to break free. I guess we'll never know.

The Dummy

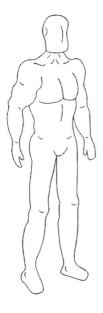

Reese turned off the TV and sat listening to the quiet. It was snowing outside, and the world was enveloped in a white blanket of silence.

A loud crash in the basement made Reese jump off the sofa and run to the top of the stairs. She opened the door and stopped, afraid to go down. Her hands shook as she fumbled with her cell phone, trying to turn on the flashlight app.

She couldn't get it to turn on. She peered into the darkness. THUMP!

She dropped the phone and ran down the hallway and

out the front door. Her fluffy slippers left odd indents in the snow. A few seconds later she was at her neighbour, banging on Graham's door.

"Reese!" he said. "What on earth? You're white as a ghost." He took her hand and pulled her inside. He led her to the sofa and sat down beside her. Her slippers left little puddles where she had stepped. "What is it? What's going on?"

"Oh, it's probably nothing," she said. "There was a noise in my basement." She was still out of breath and felt awkward as she looked down at her black and white plaid pajamas and soggy slippers. Graham put a blanket from the back of the couch over her shoulders.

Graham was fifty and had lost his wife to cancer five years earlier. Even though he was older than Reese by seventeen years, they had become friends after he helped her unload and assemble a table from IKEA when she moved into the house next door. Both were teachers and loved to read books. They had exchanged and discussed books ever since they met.

"I'll get my coat and boots and we'll go investigate together," Graham said. Reese watched him as he pulled on his winter boots and grabbed his winter coat. "Bring the blanket, you don't have a coat," he said.

Reese joined him at the door and the pair made their way back to her house.

The front door was wide open, and a small skiff of snow had accumulated in the front foyer.

"You stay here, Reese, and I'll go downstairs."

Reese tossed the blanket on a chair and followed him to the top of the basement steps. The door was still open.

At the top of the stairs she grabbed Graham's arm. "Don't you want a baseball bat or something?"

"Okay, give me the bat," he whispered back.

The pair looked down the dark narrow stairs.

"I don't have one," Reese said.

Graham gave her a quizzical look and reached for the light switch. Light flooded up from the lower level. Reese shook her head. Why hadn't she thought of that? She really was addicted to her phone.

Graham started down the stairs. Reese decided to be brave and followed close behind him, peering over his shoulder. They threaded their way through boxes, suitcases, skis, and a Christmas tree. Graham looked up at the octopus-style pipes that branched off in different directions.

"I really should organize this," Reese said.

"Hey." He held out an arm to stop her from coming closer. "What the hell is that over in the corner?"

"Oh, that. It belonged to the previous owner. The realtor said the guy would come back for it, but he never did."

"It's shaped like a man," Graham said. "A rather large man."

Sitting quietly in the corner was a densely padded black leather dummy shaped like a man. It had no defining features. Graham walked over to it and tried to pick it up. It easily weighed over a hundred pounds.

"Eerie-looking thing," he said. "Maybe it was a punching bag."

"I try to ignore it when I come down here," Reese said.

"Well, I don't see any reason for the noises you heard," Graham said, his eyes still focused on the dummy.

They looked around a bit more and then headed back upstairs.

"I'll head home then," Graham said as Reese handed him his blanket.

"I'm so sorry for interrupting your evening, Graham. It was probably something outside. Maybe the snow got too heavy and fell over, and I just thought the sound came from the basement."

Graham leaned forward and kissed her on the cheek. "You have my number. Call me if you hear anything, anything at all."

Reese felt alone as she watched him disappear into the night. She shut and locked the front door, then double-checked the lock on the back door. She was safe. It was time to get ready for bed, anyway.

As she brushed her hair and washed her face, she thought about Graham. He had a full head of hair, grey at the temples, and a beard, and often wore turtleneck sweaters that gave him the look of a professor. He was an attractive man. Reese often wished he were a little bit younger.

She crawled into bed, but sleep was not to be found. She got up and made herself a pot of herbal tea. Once it was ready, she settled in on the sofa with a book.

The house was too quiet. Even the refrigerator rested from its hum. She opened the book and decided to turn on the TV. She lowered the sound just enough to break the silence. She went back to her novel and realized the book was upside-down. She laughed at herself, turned off the TV, closed the book, grabbed her tea and went back to the bedroom. A few minutes later she was fast asleep.

Reese woke up rested, happy that it was Saturday. Every Saturday she made a fresh pot of coffee, scrambled eggs, and raspberries and toast. She savoured the taste of berries in her mouth as the aroma of fresh coffee filled the air.

After breakfast, Reese stepped out her front door to see how much snow was left in her yard. Most of it had melted, but dark clouds on the horizon promised more to come.

Across the street, the neighbour's teenage son was

checking out his bike in the driveway. He smiled and waved at her, and she smiled and waved back. Before going inside, she watched some boys playing hockey in the street. Winter was her favourite season.

Reese loved the slow pace of weekends. Dark weather made her house feel cozy. She loved the house that she had saved for and bought all by herself. It was an older brick house with built-in bookshelves around the fireplace and round archways from room to room.

She sat on the sofa with her coffee, correcting papers and contemplating her past week's work and what was to come the next week. She stood and stretched, then tidied the kitchen and stripped the bed.

She went to the basement with a basket of laundry. One by one she tossed sheets, pillowcases and towels into the washer. As the machine filled with hot water, she belted out her favourite song, "Girl On Fire" by Alicia Keys.

Reese dug the scoop down into the powdered laundry detergent. Just as she was about to pour it into the washing machine, something thudded behind her. Powdered soap flew everywhere. She turned and saw the black leather dummy lying across the bottom of the stairs. Reese screamed and froze for a moment. She wondered how the dummy had gotten way over there. It had been in the corner last night.

She looked around. There was only one exit from the

basement. She took a deep breath, laundry forgotten, ran towards the dummy, and leapt over it. One of her feet barely dragged over the densely padded form. She was out the door, still wearing slippers, in a few short seconds.

She knocked on Graham's door. He answered with a book in his hand and glasses on the end of his nose.

He looked at her with a grin. "Is that snow in your hair?"

She shook the soap flakes onto the front porch and followed him inside to the kitchen, where he poured her a cup of coffee.

"When you were over at my place yesterday, in the basement, you saw that stupid dummy over in the corner, right?" she asked before taking a sip of her coffee.

"Yes, I saw it over in the corner. Why?"

"I went downstairs to do the laundry and I didn't notice it. When I had my back turned, it somehow landed with a dead thud at the bottom of the stairs. I had to jump over the creepy thing." She shuddered at the thought and wrapped her arms around herself.

"Are you telling me it moved to another place? Impossible. There must be someone in your house, Reese." He put his coffee cup down on the table. "I'll call 911!"

"No, no," she said. "Let's not panic."

"Hey, who was at my door with soap flakes in her hair?"

Reese ignored his comment. "I can't go down there.

I'm scared. Will you come home with me?"

Graham smiled. "Of course, I will," he said.

The pair headed back to Reese's house and followed the same routine they did the night before. Reese followed closely behind Graham as they descended the narrow staircase. When they got to the bottom, the dummy was gone. Graham went over to the corner where it had been the night before. Nothing.

"It was at the bottom of the stairs, I swear," Reese said. She stood by the last step and motioned with her hands. "It was right here." She looked at Graham. He was trying to read her face. "You do believe me, don't you?"

Graham didn't answer. He put his hand on her back and gently guided her up the stairs and into the living room. He reached for a switch and turned on the fireplace. The dancing flames somehow made the room feel more comfortable, less creepy.

"Sit down, Reese." Graham motioned to the sofa, then sat down beside her. "Okay," he said. "If that dummy moved from the far corner to the bottom of the stairs, someone is or was in your house. We need to call the cops."

"But I feel like such an idiot," Reese complained.

"It's either that or try and sleep tonight knowing something weird is going on in your basement." He gave Reese a comforting squeeze on her shoulder.

"Fine," she said. "I'll call them."

Twenty minutes later, two officers showed up and were filled in on Reese's encounter with the dummy at the bottom of the stairs. They questioned Reese and Graham for forty-five minutes, as if one of them was the elusive intruder.

The officers reluctantly searched the entire house. There was no black leather man to be found anywhere. The woman was obviously delusional.

As they left, one of the officers turned to Graham and Reese. "Listen, you guys, the next time you call us, make sure there is something going on." He shook his head as he and his partner left.

Graham sat on the sofa massaging his brow. Reese paced in front of the fireplace. They were baffled.

"I do believe you, Reese. I saw the fright in your eyes. I think you'd better spend the night at my place. I'll make up a room for you. You're not safe here. Someone is playing sick games and who knows what they'll do next?"

"Thanks, Graham. What would I do without you?" She sat down beside him and he instinctively put his arm around her. She felt safe and comfortable.

After she calmed down, Graham said, "Go get what you need." He gave her a gentle nudge.

Laundry forgotten, they spent the day exploring the downtown area. They walked to the coffee shop and chatted for a bit. Then they visited their favourite bookstore and finally went shopping for dinner. Reese glanced at her house as they entered Graham's. It appeared fine, as if nothing nefarious had happened.

After dinner and a nice chat with Graham, Reese settled into the guest room. She studied the tiny flower pattern in the wallpaper. She thought about the dummy and wondered why she hadn't gotten rid of it. Why hadn't the previous owner come back for it? She was happy it was gone, but she really wanted to know who took it and who had moved it around the basement. Would they be back? Reese shivered at the thought.

She couldn't sleep and wished she had stayed up with Graham a while longer. She tossed and turned and fell into a fitful sleep, complete with disturbing dreams. She dreamed that the black leather dummy was with her, in bed. She woke with a scream. Graham heard her and rushed to her room. It was only four in the morning.

Graham stayed with Reese for a few moments to calm her down. They both knew sleep was done for the night, so they went to the kitchen and made a pot of tea. They settled down in Graham's comfy living room, drank tea, and talked. Reese examined his book collection. He had all the classics.

Daybreak came and they still sat side by side on the sofa. He asked her, "Do you have something special you would like to do someday?"

"Funny you should ask," she said. "I was just reading a travel magazine, an article on the Orient Express. I think that would be a romantic thing to do. You know, they put champagne in every cabin. How about you, Graham? What would be your dream?"

He looked off in the distance, then shifted his position on the sofa. Reese sensed he wasn't sure he wanted to say. "Come on, Graham," she said. "I told you mine."

He looked into her eyes and said, "I would like to have a child." He quickly added, "With a compatible woman, of course."

Reese was surprised by such a personal response. She had expected him to say something like skydiving, or a trip to the North Pole. She was impressed by his vulnerability.

Reese, a young healthy woman, of course thought about children in her future. The thought of having a child with Graham was not an unpleasant one. She admitted to herself that she was more comfortable with him than she had been with any other man. She'd had a few relationships, but none of them had lasted more than a year. The truth was, she'd been busy with her studies, taking extra courses, and when that was done, she aspired to be the best teacher she could be. She was devoted to her students.

There was something about Graham, though, despite his age. Whenever he was near her, close enough to smell him, she experienced light-headedness. When he would leave the last piece of pizza for her or was willing to switch seats with her at a show, she couldn't help admire his subtle gallantry.

After a week of staying with Graham, with daily checks of the house, there was no sign of the leather dummy. Reese returned home and Graham kept a close watch on her. She got back into her routine, and when it was time to do laundry, she asked Graham to check out the basement before going down herself. He found nothing.

The eerie ordeal that had brought Reese and Graham close together was over. They were so comfortable with each other that they easily fell into dating and spending time at each other's houses. One evening at dinner, Graham raised his wine glass and said, "Here's to the dummy."

Reese, who hadn't raised her glass, said, "What?"

"The catalyst that brought us closer together. I love you, Reese."

Reese's heart skipped a beat. "I love you, too, Graham."

They spent more and more time together and fell into a routine. On Saturday nights they ordered Chinese food and settled in to watch the hockey game. That particular night, the local news was on first. They were reporting on their local high school's basketball team. A comment was made on the Ravens and their odd mascot, a densely padded black leather shape of a man with no defined features. Reese and Graham moved to the edge of the sofa.

The camera scanned the bleachers and focused on a boy. It was Tony, from across the street. He sat with the strange mascot, which was wearing the team jersey and a matching ball cap.

Reese jumped off the couch. "That little devil! It was him sneaking into my house even when I was home. When I get hold of him, I'll . . ."

"Hold on, Reese!" Graham followed her as she paced in circles around the room. "Give him a chance to explain."

She looked up at him with her hands on her hips. "A chance to explain? What's to explain?" Her voice shook. "That little creep scared me half to death!"

Graham thought it was a paradox that something so eerie and strange, that had caused so much stress, could now make him smile.

"How can you smile at a time like this, Graham?"

"Sorry, I just find it funny, don't you?"

She gave him a look.

"Fine, I'll go over to his house to talk to him and his parents," Graham said.

"Not without me, you won't," Reese said.

The two of them marched across the street to the neighbour's house and knocked on the door.

Tony answered.

"My mom isn't home," he said.

"It's not your mother we want to speak to, it's you," Reese said.

"I have homework."

"Are you going to step out, or ask us in?" Graham asked.

Tony's face lost all colour. He stuttered. "W-w-well, I g-g-guess you c-c-can come in."

"I think you know why we're here, don't you?" Graham asked.

"Yeah, I figured you would be as soon as the reporters showed up at the school. I just watched the news."

"How long have you been breaking into people's homes?" Reese asked.

"I didn't break anything. I just wanted to see if it was still there. I remembered the other guy who lived there had this cool leather dummy. When he was moving he asked me to help him carry some exercise equipment upstairs. That's when I saw the dummy. He asked me if I wanted it, but I knew my folks wouldn't let me have it, so I said no. The guy said he didn't want it either and called it creepy. He told me it had been in the house when he bought it and he was leaving it."

"That's no excuse for breaking into my house!" Reese was pacing the floor again.

"I know, I know. I had told my friends about the dummy and they asked me if it was still there. You were out and I snuck in through the basement window. Then you came home and I was trapped down there. When I tried to climb out the window, I knocked over the lamp. It was all good, it didn't break or anything. Then I told my friends it was still there. They told the rest of the team and they said I should ask you for it, to be our team mascot."

"So, why didn't you just ask me?" Reese asked. "I would have happily given it to you." Reese slowed her pacing to a walk around the living room.

Tony shrugged.

Reese stopped in front of him. "And how the heck did you get it to the stairs?"

"We snuck in through the window again, but then you came down to do laundry. While you were singing and the water was running, we made a break for it and got the dummy all the way to the top of the stairs. Then we lost our grip and it slid down to the bottom. We hid in the front closet and a few seconds later you went running out. When we figured you would be gone for a while, we dragged it out the cellar window over the laundry tub."

"I thought that window was sealed and locked," Reese said. She stood, hands on her hips, staring Tony down. "Where is it now?" she asked.

"It's in our basement." Tony motioned to the basement door. "My friend and I put it there after last night's game. My mom saw it and freaked out. She said I had to get rid of it, she didn't want it in her house. When Dad came home, I had to tell him how we got it. He was really mad. He said he was going to take it to the dump tomorrow. If it makes you feel any better, I'm grounded for two weeks. I was going to come over tomorrow and tell you everything and apologize. I really am sorry. I never meant to scare you."

Reese was relieved that the mystery was solved. She understood peer pressure, but he wasn't going to get away with it that easily. "Aside from being grounded, I want you and your friend to come over tomorrow and help me organize the entire basement. Is that clear? Then we're even."

"Yes, ma'am," Tony said. "We'll be there at nine a.m."

"Good, and bring garbage bags. Your dad can take more than that dummy to the dump."

Graham put his arm on Reese's shoulder. "I think we should go now."

"Tomorrow. Nine a.m. Be there," Reese said as she pointed at Tony.

The couple walked back over to Reese's, hand in hand. "Well, that's that," she said.

"Yup, that's that," Graham said as they walked into the living room and flopped onto the sofa, laughing.

The next day, the boys helped organize her basement, with more apologies from both of them. Tony's dad came over and helped haul out the garbage bags. He assured Reese that Tony would never do anything like that again, and the garbage and the dummy would be in the dump by sunset.

Reese was exhausted. She was about to step into the shower when Graham phoned.

"Is it all done?" he asked.

"Yes, all of it cleaned and organized, and the garbage hauled away. Now I need a hot shower."

"Well, once you've showered, dress warmly and come over. I want to take you somewhere."

"Where are we going?" Reese asked.

"It's a surprise. Dress warm and I'll see you in a bit."

Reese hopped into the shower, the water washing away the sweat of the morning. She blow-dried her hair, put on pants and a sweater, grabbed her coat and headed over to Graham's.

"Where are we going?" she asked.

Graham just smiled.

Ten minutes later they pulled up in front of an outdoor skating rink. Graham rented them skates and helped Reese get hers on.

"Why are you so good to me?" she asked.

"Because you deserve it," he answered.

After a few spins around the rink, Reese tripped and fell on her bottom. She was laughing hard when Graham skated up beside her.

"Hey, you, I'm the one who should be down there." Graham helped Reese back up on her skates and got down on one knee. He took a small box from his jacket pocket. Reese gasped.

"After meeting you, becoming your friend, spending time with you, getting to know you, and loving you, I can't imagine my life without you. Will you marry me?"

Reese's heart beat fast and a tear of joy trickled down her face. "Yes," she said. "Yes, I will."

She threw herself at him and the pair toppled onto their backs in the middle of the skating rink. Through tears of laughter, Graham placed the ring on her finger. Reese stared at it, and then at Graham.

"I may not be able to take you on the Orient Express for our honeymoon, but I can promise you champagne," he said.

"That will be perfect," Reese said as the pair got up and skated into their future together.

The Decision

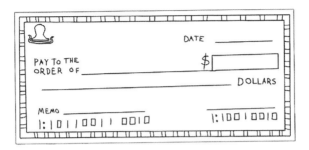

After twenty-three years of marriage, I discovered our relationship wasn't what I believed it to be. I found this out after Erick's death. I told him many times not to use that damn cell phone while driving. Now I can't confront him as to why he, a wealthy man, left me, his wife, with nothing. Everything was left to his twenty-five-year-old daughter, Lydia, from a previous marriage.

Lydia had lived with her mother growing up. When she was a young girl, she spent every second weekend, and holidays, with us. We got along well enough, more like a household dog and cat—we respected each other.

"Joanna," Lydia said to me in the lawyer's office after the reading of the will. "Don't worry. If there's anything you need, just ask me." She walked out of the office with an air of superiority. The lawyer offered me a glass of water.

Now, there I was, forty-three-years old, and I had to depend on that girl to support me. 'Just ask me,' she said.

She gave me permission to stay in *her house*. The house was in her name. I had been living in her house all along.

I told myself I would never ask her for anything. But what would I do? Where would I go? I grabbed Erick's picture and screamed at him. *How could you do this to me? I thought you loved me. I know you did. So why?*

My friends all said, "Sue the bitch. Take her to court." To be honest, I don't know why I didn't. Was I playing the victim? I don't think so. I was in so much psychological pain that I couldn't think straight. Maybe the universe had another plan for me. Time would tell.

Pain turned to anger. I stayed in the bedroom most of the time in my pyjamas. I ranted and raved out loud and on paper.

I carried on like that for a month, until the morning Lydia called to say she had made arrangements to have the house painted. I loved this pale-yellow house with white trim. It would now be teal blue with navy trim. I had no say. My life as I knew it was over.

I packed my designer suitcases with my designer clothes and jewelry. I filled several shopping bags. As I sat in the front seat of the taxi with my belongings in the back, I was numb.

"Where to, lady?"

"As far from this neighbourhood as a hundred and fifty dollars will take me." That was all I had. All credit had been frozen.

The driver sighed. "East or west?"

"You pick," I said.

As I sat in the taxi, I watched solid brick homes with manicured lawns and flower gardens graduate into the suburbs. Then it was strip mall after strip mall. People on the street were going about their lives. I wondered if any of them were going about life with a broken heart. My skirt and tank top stuck to me. All the windows in the cab were open and the humidity was stifling. The cabbie apologized for the lack of AC.

I had no plan. In a moment of panic, I almost told him to take me back. But there was panic back there, too. I was in limbo, between a world of controlled security and the unknown. My palms were wet, my head spun, and my heart thumped under my ribs. As the meter clicked over to $115, I thought I might vomit. I didn't. I looked out the window and saw a flashing sign: PAWN SHOP.

"Stop!" I yelled.

The driver slammed on the brakes. "For Christ's sake, lady!"

"Wait here," I said. I grabbed the black velvet bag that held my jewelry. I ran into the shop and traded a twelve-thousand-dollar ring for two thousand dollars.

I spent the night in a motel going over my past and cursing Erick. "Should I hate a dead man?" I asked myself.

No, I didn't hate him, I loved him. I missed him so much. It was the not knowing I hated. All those years didn't make sense to me now. Everyone said our marriage was perfect. We travelled abroad and spent time in New York. I saw and experienced places and things I never would have otherwise. The best part was having the experience with Erick.

But in spite of that life, a question about finances sometimes floated around the edges of my mind. I had a generous monthly allowance and I shopped with the other society ladies, but I rarely used it all. Every spring and fall, I donated bags of clothes, price tags and all, to women's shelters.

It wasn't about the money. Huge amounts of money made me uncomfortable and I was happy Erick took care of it. It was just that I felt left out of something important. Other wives knew about their financial status. Over the years, I had asked a few times about our finances and was told not to worry—it was all taken care of.

The only thing I felt was really mine was my writing. I had a column in the local paper. I wrote for free until it became popular and the paper started to pay me. Of course, it was a pittance, but in my mind, it validated me as a writer.

I pawned more jewelry and sold my clothes but kept my wedding ring set. I got a job in the mail room of a large newspaper. The small apartment I rented became my sanctuary. It came with a bed, a sofa and a kitchen table. I shopped at flea markets and garage sales, where I found white sheer drapes, an oriental rug and a desk. After hanging the drapes myself, I danced on the rug. At the end of the month, I paid my rent and utilities and bought my own groceries. It was the first time in my life I was responsible for me.

I began to write a novel at my new desk. It was something I had wanted to do forever. I wasn't angry anymore, but I still wondered why I wasn't in the will and what Erick had been thinking.

One year passed and I still looked at Erick's picture every day. One fall morning, my favourite time of year, I went for a walk. The magic of the coloured leaves and the chill in the air exhilarated me in my new life. I'd been given a promotion at work and a pay raise. I was as far from my old life as could be. That feeling was dampened when I thought I saw Lydia duck down a side street. I convinced myself that she was not the only woman in Toronto with long blond hair. And what would Lydia be doing in this neighbourhood anyway?

That evening, I released Erick and recycled his photo. The next day I gave my engagement and wedding rings to a young man at work who was going to propose to his girlfriend when he'd saved enough money to buy a set of rings.

As life would have it, there are always surprises. In late November, on a Sunday morning, I was doing yoga before settling down to write. There was a knock on my apartment door. I was expecting to see Julia from across the hall. Her timing was always off.

I opened the door and there stood Lydia. We looked at each other and waited to see who would speak first. It wasn't me. I turned and walked away, leaving the door open.

She entered and closed the door behind her. I sat on the sofa in my workout clothes, my hair gathered on top of my head in a bun. I watched her. Without being invited, she sat in a chair opposite me. I saw her eyes dart around the apartment and I wondered what she thought. She wore a pink Armani suit and very high heels. I remembered asking her one time why she was always dressed up. She said it gave her confidence.

It seemed like hours before she spoke. She had a perfectly placed mole above the corner of mouth and I often found that to be my focus when she was speaking. Not today.

"I need to talk to you, Joanna." She fidgeted with her keys. I didn't reply. She placed a black bag at her feet and swept her hair off her shoulders with a toss of her head.

I folded my arms and crossed my legs, a thread of resentment stirring in me. I thought I'd dealt with that, but apparently not. It wasn't about the money. I felt like she and her family didn't care what happened to me. It hurt.

"Did you know Dad kept a journal?" She spoke in a gentle voice—unusual for her.

"No. Well, he did say something about how he keeps track of everything in a book. But I never gave it much thought. I figured it was all work-related."

"Yes, work-related, but also personal. He wrote in it at work in the mornings before he began his day. The office gave me a box of personal things from his desk. I had it for six months before I opened it."

She stood and walked to the window. With her back to me, she said, "I've been watching you, Joanna, the last couple of days."

"You've been stalking me?"

She turned around and said, "No, not stalking. I've been trying to get the courage to approach you. I saw how happy you were with your new life. Please believe me when I say I'm happy for you."

I didn't care how she felt. I wanted to know about the book she found. "What about Erick's journal?"

"Journals—there was more than one. I brought them with me." She sat down, reached into the black bag and took them out. She put them on the coffee table. There were six black hardcover journals with red bindings.

"You can read them, but I want to tell you the important part myself."

I felt nervous, not knowing what I was about to hear.

Lydia's lips moved as if she was trying to formulate a sentence. "First thing is, I had no idea Dad planned to leave everything to me. I was taken aback by this, and I knew it wasn't right, but I convinced myself that this was what he wanted. I found out from his journals that when Mom divorced him, she got half of his fortune. Shortly after, she married my stepdad. He took control of my mom's money and gambled it away. Dad was very upset about that."

"That explains why he left me with nothing," I said. "Now I know why. He didn't trust me."

Lydia leaned forward. "Maybe he didn't in the beginning, Joanna. He'd been burnt once. But when you read his journals, you'll see that he loved you more than anyone. I think you know Dad was in the habit of making notes and dating them. His reminders. Some were tucked into his journals. They hadn't been written in yet." She passed me a yellow Post-it note. "This was between the pages of his last writing."

It said:

Call my lawyer, Hank, and make new will. Should have done this long ago. Half and half to the two most important girls in my life.

I let the revelation sink in. He loved and cared about me.

"That's you and me, Joanna." She leaned back in the chair. "Please forgive me for the way I acted. It was immature of me. I was never happy about it, though. It just didn't feel right. So, after reading his journals and finding this note, I'm in the process of liquidating all assets."

She took a plain white envelope from her purse and put it on the table. "This is a start, and the rest will follow when it's available." She got up and stood by the door with her hand on the knob. "Oh, by the way, his old will was made before he met you. Same with the house. He bought it after he and Mom divorced."

She opened the door and left.

I went to the front window and watched her cross the street to her car. She looked up at my window and raised her hand. I raised mine.

I opened the envelope after she left. A certified check for five million dollars.

I had no feeling about the money one way or the other. I left it on the coffee table. I ignored it for a while, but then I had to decide what to do with it. It was a weekend. I thought about Erick all Saturday and Sunday. I read the journals and took comfort in the fact that Erick's and my relationship was as I originally thought, and maybe more so.

On Monday morning on my way to work, I stopped at my favourite coffee shop.

"Hi, Joanna. The usual?" Anne asked, the girl taking orders.

"Yes," I answered with a smile.

In my hand I held an envelope addressed to Lydia. I took my coffee to go, walked straight to the mailbox and dropped the envelope in. I was satisfied with my self-supporting life. Self-supporting—that was the key word. The feeling was priceless.

One More Time

Patricia Smith was exactly what I needed after my ex-wife took our son and moved to Winnipeg. I met her at my company's convention. Out-of-town people were there from our sister company, so we all had name tags. Except Patricia. She really knew how to work a room with a kind of catwalk saunter that oozed sexuality—natural or practiced, I wasn't sure. I watched as the other men competed for her attention and the women whispered.

The room was pretty full. I had arrived late and gotten the last table by the door. She came over and gestured to an empty chair. I stood and pulled it out for her. She sat, leaned forward, and fingered a silver pendant that hung around her neck. Her red silk blouse matched her lipstick.

"Ron?" she said as she extended her hand.

"You know my name?" I said as I shook hers.

"It's on your name tag. I'm Patricia."

I let her hand go and struggled to redeem myself. "I haven't seen you around here before."

"This is my first day. My husband transferred out here to another company and I got hired on by yours."

The word 'husband' was disappointing.

"So, you're married?" I asked.

"Yes," she said, and adjusted her brown hair over her shoulder.

"Children?" I asked.

"Two. A boy, twelve, and a girl, eight. And you?"

"Divorced, one son. He's with his mother in Winnipeg. And you like horses."

"How did you know?" she asked.

"The horse engraved on your pendant," I said as I pointed with my eyes.

We laughed like giddy teenagers for the rest of the night. I was already feeling hopeful. We didn't pay much attention to the program, or the speeches, or the videos. That night there was only us.

When I got home that night, I looked in the mirror, finger-combed my thinning hair, and thought I should update my glasses. I wondered if I looked my age: forty-nine. Patricia was thirty-two. I told myself to run, run like I was on fire. She was married with two kids, for Christ's sake. Who does that? I had been thinking about giving up my lucrative job and my lonely apartment and moving to be closer to my son. But then I met Patricia. The excitement I felt inside was impossible to resist. I felt young.

We started off sitting together in the work lunchroom. Later on, on our coffee breaks, we would meet at a coffee shop across the street from work. Our toes would meet under the table and linger there. Neither of us pulled away. Our hands would be side by side on the table, nearly touching.

I was the first to make the move. I turned her hand over and stroked her palm. She responded with a smile and put her hand on mine. There began our relationship.

On Thursdays, I would leave the office for the forty-five-minute drive to my cabin set among the white birch trees. It had been my family's cabin and we spent most of our summers there. When my parents passed away and my sister moved to Europe, I acquired the cabin. It was my get-away retreat when I needed to have a break from apartment living. It was the perfect place for Patricia and I to meet without being noticed.

Patricia would follow half an hour later. Our weekly passion-filled evenings were all we had, and we made the most of them. We fed each other sweet grapes on the rug in front of the fire. Then I would take her hand, help her up, and carry her to the bedroom.

We breathed in unison. Our spirits were united in our embrace.

"My God, Patricia, I love you," I said.

She wrapped herself around me in an embrace that owned me. We kissed long and hard with a passion that brought me to dizzying heights. I adored her calling out my name. I felt her fingers dig deep into my back.

Afterwards, we would satisfy our appetites with the dinner I had brought. I finally asked where her husband thought she was every Thursday evening.

"He thinks I go to the library to work on my poetry. Tuesday evening is his turn to be out. He has beers with the boys from work."

We kept our distance at work. In the lunchroom she sat at another table, though always in my line of vision. She would eat grapes, sucking them in one by one. I tried not to look. We carried on like this for two and a half months.

It was Wednesday, and the first December snow put me in a sentimental mood. I was looking forward to the next day when Patricia called from her office to mine.

"I can't do this anymore," she said in a whisper. "I might lose my family. I missed my daughter's dance recital, and last week I missed my son's soccer game. They won the trophy and I wasn't there."

"Slow down, Patricia. Slow down. Let's talk about this." I couldn't lose her, not now.

"No, Ron. My mind's made up. I think my husband's suspicious. He asked to see my poetry and I didn't have much to show him. I just can't do this anymore. I'm nervous all the time. What if he checks out the library tomorrow?"

"What about us? It's fate. We were meant to be."

"Well, damn it, Ron, fate messed up. Got the timing all wrong. Please try to understand. It's hard enough. The thought of losing my kids . . ." her voice trailed off and I could hear her breathing through the phone.

I began to pace around the office. I closed the Venetian blinds so no one could see how stressed I was. "I do understand. I do. But we can't cut it off just like that. Can't we meet one more time? Come early—then you can leave early and get to the library."

There was a long pause.

"Patricia, are you there?" I stopped pacing. "Patricia!"

"Okay, Ron, one more time. I'll bring wine."

"I'll bring dinner," I said.

On Thursday, I sat at my computer trying to look busy. It was useless. I was overcome with a sense of sadness and feeling antsy. I set out early for the cabin, as planned. I stopped at the deli and picked up a roast chicken, Patricia's favourite salad, and a loaf of French bread.

It began to snow as I arrived at the cabin. I made a fire and stood at the window watching for her. My heart beat faster when I saw her red Toyota drive around the curve of the birch-lined driveway. I opened the door and stepped out onto the veranda to greet her. She ran into my arms and I held her as snowflakes clung to her eyelashes.

"I really shouldn't be here," she said as she stomped the snow off her boots. Her dark eyes grew darker. I could see she was anxious.

We sat by the fire as a grey cloud hovered over us. My heart felt as heavy as a stone. We made love right there on the rug. Afterwards, we didn't have our usual appetite, we just nibbled at the food.

I held her hand across the table. "Patricia, are you sure this is what you want?"

"For God's sake, Ron. It's not about what I want."

"Couldn't we just change things up a bit? Meet at different times? I could give up my Saturday basketball or my Monday night card game."

She shook her head and stood. When she went to the door to put on her boots and parka, I knew it was over. She kissed my cheek, squeezed my hand and left, shutting the door behind her.

I closed up the cabin and wondered if I should sell and make the move I had been thinking about. I wondered if she would ever come back to me. Probably not.

As I drove down the dark highway, I had to slow and then stop. Some sort of traffic jam. I didn't mind. I wasn't in a hurry to get home to my empty apartment. I turned off the radio and sat in silence. I studied the tiny patterns of the snowflakes as they perched on my wipers. I tried to take my mind off her. I didn't want to think.

The traffic started to move. As we rounded a curve, I saw an eighteen-wheeler on its side. I figured it was probably some idiot going too fast for the road conditions. I hoped Patricia was ahead of the accident. She'd had an hour's head start.

The traffic was now reduced to one lane, alternating north- and south-bound and still moving at a crawl. I broke into a sweat when I saw a tow truck hoisting a small red car onto its bed. The traffic, already slow, stopped again. I jumped out of my car, leaving the door open. I ran to the scene, slipped on the ice and almost fell. An ambulance was parked off to the side with lights flashing.

"Is she in there?" I yelled at a cop as I made my way towards the ambulance. "The driver, is she in there?"

Now there was an officer on either side of me, holding me by the arms. "What's your name?" one of them asked.

"Ron! My name is Ron!"

"Is she your wife, Ron?"

I hesitated. "My girlfriend. She's my girlfriend!" I

turned in a circle, pushing their hands away from me. They grabbed my arms again. Another officer stood in front of me. I breathed out fear.

"She's not in there," he said.

I looked at him, puzzled. "Where is she?" The two cops held me tighter. "Where is she?" I yelled again.

He pointed to the coroner's van. Through the still-falling snow, I saw them loading in a dark green body bag. My legs gave out. I was on my knees.

"It's my fault!" I called out to the body bag. "I did this to you, Patricia. I'm so sorry. I just wanted one more time." Icy tears streamed down my cheeks.

They pulled me up. I wanted to see her. I was afraid to see her. My stomach twisted as they walked with me to the coroner's van and its doors slammed shut.

A woman stood by the van, speaking into a recorder.

". . . female pronounced dead at the scene."

My knees felt weak again.

She continued, "Driver's license says age nineteen. Name: Ann Marie Johnston."

I took a deep breath and let out a sigh of relief.

I watched the van drive away as the lightly falling snow reflected the blue and red flashing lights. I turned and went back to my car.

I continued to drive home. I missed my son. I'd start looking for a new job tomorrow.

Bill and Harry: A Conversation

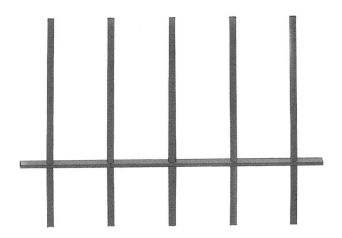

Bill leapt off his upper bunk and gripped the iron bars with both hands. "I know exactly what I'll do when I get out of this hellhole," he said. "Twenty-nine more days to go. Yep, I know exactly what I'll do."

"Tell me, Bill," Harry said, his cellmate. "What are you gonna do?"

"Well, Harry, I have one thing in mind. I'll stand outside of my wife's house and stare at the window. Give them the look, you know. I won't say a word, just stare. I'll stare at that son of a bitch who took my place. He set me up, you know. That's why I'm in here. Then he moves in with *my wife*, into *my house*. He even walks *my dog*. Yeah, I have my sources out there."

Bill was pacing now, five steps one way and five steps back. Harry was stretched out on the lower bunk. Bill stopped to glare at him, to give him a better idea of the look he had in mind: eyes squinted, eyebrows low, mouth tight, and fists clenched.

"The next day I'll do the same thing, but from the other side of the street. Just stare like I'm crazy. To freak them out, you know. No law against standing on the sidewalk that I know of. Do you?"

Harry shook his head. He swung his legs over the side of his bunk and sat up. "No, but there is against harassment."

Bill ignored that. He ran his fingers through his hair as he glanced sideways into the dull mirror above the sink and stroked his beard.

"What else do you have in mind, Bill?"

"Well, I know where they shop every Saturday morning. They always shop together, and guess what, that will be my shopping day, too. They'll see me everywhere. By coincidence, of course." He grinned, exposing one gold tooth. "I won't say a word. Just glare." He practiced the look in the mirror. His belly shook with laughter.

"You know what, Bill?" Harry said. "You'll soon be out of here, but you're gonna land right back in if you don't smarten up."

"Okay, wise guy, then tell me what you're gonna do

when you get out."

"One thing's for sure," Harry said. "I don't plan on coming back to this place. Nope. I've learned my lesson." He gestured at the picture on the wall. "See that little girl? My life will be to do right by her. Make her proud." He touched the photo. "She's only three. I'm hoping her mother hasn't told her about my stay here."

Bill looked over Harry's shoulder. "Nice-looking kid. But the mother? Good luck with that. Women! So, what's your plan, wise guy? You're not far behind me and you'll be free, too."

"Well, first," Harry said, "I'll get a job in a hospital." He leaned his back against the bars. "I wanted to be a nurse. I had two years of school behind me when I landed in here. So, I'll continue on with my studies."

Bill couldn't contain himself. "A nurse!" The slap he landed on Harry's shoulder almost knocked him over. "I thought you said a nurse." He put a hand over his mouth to muffle his laugh. It was Harry's turn to glare.

"Okay, okay! Sorry. This is getting interesting." Bill flopped onto Harry's bunk, folded his arms and crossed his ankles. "I'm listening."

Harry continued. "I'll try to quit smoking. I'm cutting back already. It'll be easy because I'll be busy. My mom was a nurse. She said they always want more male nurses. I remember when I was in hospital with pneumonia, I had a nurse who was so nice to me. I never forgot, and I decided then and there, that's what I wanted to be."

"I'll bet she was a cutie, eh?"

"Shut up, Bill. Tell me the rest of your smartass plan."

Bill was silent as he examined his fingernails. "I don't want to land back in here either. I might move away, start fresh, you know. Find a focus for myself, you know, a good job."

"Good," Harry said. "Good. That's the attitude. I'm glad you see the light. Move on and forward. Why don't you look into a trade school?"

"Yeah, but you know, schools are expensive, and those teachers are losers. I could teach them a thing or two. But I'll think about it. My so-called dad was a plumber. Wouldn't want to do that. But I always kinda liked welding. Yeah, maybe I'll be a welder."

"Great trade. Glad to see you're making a constructive plan for your future. A new start somewhere else will make all the difference."

"Yeah, you're right, Harry. A new town, a new start. And if I do move, I can still bug them. I'll send a large picture of myself, one a week, with that glare I showed you."

He laughed so hard tears rolled down his face. "Yep, one picture a week. They won't be able to forget me. I won't let them." He jumped up. "I got it! I know what

I'll do." He grinned a wide grin. "I got a car stored at my brother's place."

"Yeah?"

"I'll sell it." Bill paced back and forth, nodding. "Yeah. I'll sell it," he said, stroking his beard.

"Good. You'll have some money for your welding course."

"Nah, the government will pay for that."

"I'm afraid to ask. What will you do with the money?"

"I'm gonna rent one of those damned billboards. You know, the annoying ones on the side of the highway coming into town. Can't help but look at them. They'll see me every time they go to work. Bigger than life. With that look! Yup, I'll be glaring at them and my eyes will follow them."

Harry gave a deep sigh, lay back on his bunk, and shook his head. "Hopeless," he muttered.

Granny Rose's Message

When James Anderson arrived home from a night out on the town with his girlfriend, Sophie Sanders, he sensed someone was in his apartment. It was the unfamiliar scent in the air.

He glanced around and everything seemed in place. After a cautious walk around, he heard the sound of someone clearing their throat. Then he saw her. It was Rose McDonald, his late grandmother.

She sat by the fireplace in one of the matching wing-back chairs, which she had swivelled around to face him. She looked smaller than he remembered, but she still had curly hair and glasses, and her light blue sweatsuit and matching fluffy mule slippers were typical for her. She held her cane between her knees, with her hands, one over the other, resting on it.

He stared at the translucent apparition before saying, "Granny

Rose! What are you doing here?"

"Where are your manners, young man? Aren't you going to say hello to me?" She tapped her cane on the floor.

James, feeling a bit weak in the knees, moved to the window seat a safe distance away. He had never seen a ghost before.

"How can you be here, Granny Rose?"

"Now, you just never mind, James, as to how. You need to ask why."

James was silent for a moment. He wasn't sure he wanted to know why. He looked at the floor, rubbed his neck and eyes, and looked up. She was still there.

"Okay, Granny, tell me. Why?"

"First, I want to say, that girlfriend of yours, Sophie, she's a keeper. She's a good girl who loves you." She shook a finger at him. "Make it work this time."

"You know about her?"

"Of course, I know about her. I keep an eye on things around here."

"Oh, really?" James got up, moved to the other side of the room, and leaned against the bookshelves.

"Don't worry. You get your privacy."

James laughed and relaxed a little. "Okay, are you going to tell me why you're here, Granny?"

"James, come sit here." She gestured with her cane to

the chair on the other side of the fireplace.

James obliged and sat facing his grandmother. "Do you still need that cane over there—up there—down . . .?"

"Of course not. But when we present ourselves to people here, we appear as they remember us. So they know who we are. Now, James, we must get down to business. You know your cousin, Gary."

"Yes, Granny. I just saw him a few days ago. He was on his way to Goodwill. He said he was getting rid of stuff. He stopped at Starbucks and picked up a coffee to go. I walked out with him and noticed his van was full. Out of the blue, he asked me if I wanted his iPhone. I thought that was odd. I told him I already had one."

"Yes, yes, I know," Granny said. "He is getting his house in order. He rents it, so he wouldn't want his landlord to have to deal with his stuff. James, I have to tell you this. Gary plans to commit suicide on Saturday."

"Gary? No! He seemed so relaxed, so happy. Suicide? No."

"Yes, Gary has planned his suicide. I'll tell you this, James. When a person is so depressed and they want to end it all, they see suicide as the only way out. When that decision is made, they feel relieved, happy even. He blames himself for the accident that killed Jenny and Jodi. Losing his wife and daughter in a car accident when he was driving … well, that's too much for him to deal with."

She shook her head in sympathy. "He doesn't know that it was their time, but not his. So, on Saturday, he plans to jump off the bridge."

"What should I do? What *can* I do?"

"You must figure it out yourself. I wouldn't put this on you, James, if you couldn't do it." Her voice trailed off and her apparition faded away.

James couldn't sleep that night. He wasn't a psychologist or a therapist of any kind. What could he do to help his cousin? He considered putting this bizarre experience down to a dream, or his imagination, or just forget it happened. He didn't believe in ghosts or the afterlife. But it *had* happened. Would Granny Rose's ghost come back to reprimand him if he didn't at least try to help? Of course not. But what if . . .?

The next morning James called Gary. It seemed Gary's phone had been disconnected, so James went to his cousin's house. He coaxed his apprehensive body down the walkway and up two steps to the townhouse door. He raised a hesitant fist and knocked. He heard someone moving around inside.

"Gary. Are you there? It's James. I need to talk to you." He knocked again.

James heard footsteps. The door opened. Gary stood there stroking a cat he held in his arms. "Hey, James. Come in. Something wrong?"

James hadn't really noticed before how much they looked like each other. They both resembled their fathers, who were brothers. Gary had ash-blond hair and blue eyes like James, except Gary's hair was thinning at the front and he wore glasses. If there had been a reason to smile here, their perfect teeth and smiles would have been exactly the same.

James searched for words. His eyes scanned the mostly vacant living room. A TV, surrounded by wires, sat on the floor in the corner. A kitchen chair was in front of it.

"So, you really are cleaning out. But totally?" He followed Gary to the kitchen and noticed the cupboard doors were wide open, revealing their empty interiors. An opened bag of cat food and a couple of half-full paper coffee cups sat on the counter.

Aware of James taking visual notes, Gary said, "I'm going away, and since you're here, I have a favour to ask of you." Still holding the cat, he motioned his arms forward. "Jake here, he needs a home. I don't want to give him to the SPCA. Too many cats there."

"Hey—wait a minute. How long are you going for?"

Gary put Jake down. With his hands in his pockets, he looked at the floor. "I can't say."

"Well, for Christ's sake. You've gotten rid of everything. All that's left is an empty house. What's going on? Looks like you're never coming back."

"I suppose you wouldn't be satisfied if I asked you to let me be and take Jake?" Gary opened the fridge and grabbed a carton of milk. He filled Jake's dish.

"No, I wouldn't," James said. "I know we haven't been that close, you and me, only seeing each other at family get-togethers and all. The last time was at the . . ." James felt guilty. He hadn't visited Gary since the funeral. There were other people in the family who had been there to help. Like Aunt Connie—she was always the first at the door of a bereaved relative with a pie or a cake. James's own mom had helped with the funeral arrangements. He'd planned to visit—he just kept putting it off. What does a person say at a time like this? Six months had passed.

"Well, why the hell are you here now, James? Why now?" Gary kicked the garbage can. He moved to the living room and sat on the floor. Tears streamed down his face like he was a wounded child.

James sat on the lone chair. "Gary, come on. What's going on? Talk to me."

"Please take the cat and go." Gary's chest heaved.

"No. I know what you're planning, Gary, and I won't let you do it." James was in it now. No backing away. He was genuinely concerned about his cousin. He had abandoned his sense of not wanting to get involved.

"What do you know? We hardly know each other. Just get out of here and take Jake with you."

His sobbing was now uncontrollable.

"Take the damn cat. He's Jodi's cat. I can't mess that up, too. Promise me, no SPCA. That's all I ask. Please."

James stood, lunged forward and grabbed Gary by the arm. "Get up off the floor. Stand up! I know what you're planning. Yeah, on Saturday you plan to jump off the Okanagan floating bridge." His face was as red as Gary's now.

Gary stared at James. "How in the hell would you know that?"

"Granny Rose told me."

There was silence. The two men stood staring each other in the eyes.

"What?" Gary said.

"Yeah, sounds strange, I know."

"Strange . . . yeah. Granny Rose is dead." Gary stopped crying. His face was all blotchy and wet. "What's wrong with you, James? Why would you say that? Have you gone weird or something?"

"I know, I know. But it's true. She said you must not leave here. It was Jenny and Jodi's time. Not yours. She said she is with them in a wonderful place. Jenny wants you to stop grieving. If you do that, they will be able to move on. Jodi wants you to stay here and take care of Jake."

James was just as surprised as Gary as the words came

out of his mouth. Was Granny Rose speaking through him? He didn't know this much about the afterlife.

Gary responded, "What do you mean . . . move on?"

"Grieving holds them close to the earth. You must let them go," James said, still wondering how he knew these things. "There's an even better place than where they are now. That's all I know."

Gary went to the kitchen sink, splashed his face with cold water and dried it with a paper towel. A few minutes passed before the two men spoke.

"Is it really possible that Granny Rose came back from the dead with a message?" Gary asked. "I never believed in that shit."

"Me neither, but I saw her with my own eyes, cane and all, sitting in my living room."

"I need some air. Let's go outside."

They sat on the patio for the rest of the afternoon and talked about life, death, and the Blue Jays. James ordered pizza.

As James was leaving, Gary said, "We should get together for coffee, or better yet, a beer."

"Okay," James said. "How about Saturday?"

"Deal." Gary extended his hand. They shook on the plan.

The two cousins met that Saturday at a local pub. They drank beer and talked about their lives. For a second,

James caught a glimpse of a smiling Granny Rose sitting in a corner booth. She raised her cane, nodded, and faded away.

Don't Think Pink

Anthony McKinney paced back and forth in the vestry of St. Michael's Catholic Church. He was dressed in a tuxedo, pink cummerbund and all. It was minutes before the wedding ceremony that would marry him to Melody.

The organ played the music Melody had picked. It mixed in with the muffled voices of the guests as they filled the seats. The smell of incense and furniture polish in the church was familiar to him. He had grown up in this church, as had his entire family. His parents, grandparents, older sister, and cousins all had successful marriages, and they had all started at St. Michael's. This gave the church a great reputation. "Married at St. Mike's, it's sure to go right," his grandmother would often say.

Even though he hated pink, he should've been able to

deal with the cummerbund and pink bowtie. The whole damn wedding was pink, from the invitations to the flowers, from the eight bridesmaids' dresses to the stretch limo. He hated pink.

Anthony's thoughts drifted back to his childhood. He could see his boyhood room in his mind. There were bicycle magazines scattered on his bed and posters of bikes on the wall. At the head of his bed was a life-sized poster of his dream bike. It was a red BMX, loaded with the latest in pedals, wheels, and state-of-the-art handlebars. Oh, how he dreamed about that bike.

On his birthday, his dad took him to a bike shop. He was told he could pick out any bike he wanted.

Anthony could hardly contain himself with the excitement of the moment as they entered the store. The exact bike he wanted was featured on a platform in the middle of all the other bikes. Except it wasn't red. It was pink. He sat down on the floor in front of it as if to pay homage.

The salesman approached with a smile. "Well, son, I see you know a great bike when you see it."

"He has a poster of this bike, but it's red," his dad said.

"This pink one is all we have in stock right now, but I'll see what we have in the warehouse."

When the salesman returned, he told them the bikes were on back order and it would be a month to six weeks before he had the other colours in.

Anthony's dad told the man they could wait.

"Or maybe," he said to Anthony, "you can pick out something else. There are a lot of bikes here."

"Ohhhh, man," Anthony said as he put both hands on his head, closed his eyes, shifted on his feet. He looked at the bike again. "No, it's okay, Dad. I'll take the pink one. I'll take it."

"Are you sure, son? If we buy it, you'll have to ride it. Are you sure you don't want to wait? Are you sure you want pink?"

Anthony recalled that summer and the merciless teasing from the other boys, who called him Suzie.

"Hey, Suzie," Jamie had said. "My sister will loan you her ribbons."

He rode that pink bike with his head held high, knowing it really was the best BMX bike in town. Whenever he rode it, he would say to himself, *don't think pink, don't think pink.* Halfway through the summer, thinking Anthony had suffered enough, his dad had the bike professionally painted red.

As an adult, an abundance of pink still made Anthony queasy. Melody knew the significance of pink to him. The story had been told over and over at family gatherings. But a pink wedding had been her dream ever since she was a little girl.

"Get over it, Anthony," was her response when he protested. She would not give in. So, Anthony gave in, as he had many times before—or was that every time?

Like the honeymoon. He'd had his heart set on Scotland, the land of his ancestors. But Melody wanted a Caribbean cruise, so she booked it and told Anthony it was done. "I bought three pink bikinis," she had said. "I couldn't wear them in Scotland." Then she flipped her blond hair over her shoulder.

Anthony had brushed these things off as not important. But would he ever have a say in anything? Was he so in love that he had become gullible and naïve? His sister had called him gullible once. She'd said, "I don't know why some people just don't get it when everybody else does." Anthony had shrugged her comment off at the time. Why was he thinking about it now?

He rubbed his neck as he wondered about his choice in brides. *Does Melody really love me? Do I love her just for her beauty, her sexiness? Do I even know her?* They had only been together six months when she proposed to him. All this pink was making him a little crazy.

Anthony stood with his hands behind his back as he looked out the window of the vestry. Jason, his best man, came in, tapped him on the shoulder, and broke his train of thought. "It's time, buddy."

When Anthony didn't respond, Jason repeated, "It's

time. Time to stand at the altar. Can't you hear the music? Melody's about to come down the aisle. The groomsmen are all lined up."

"Jason, don't ask me any questions. Just go get Melody and bring her in here."

"Anthony? What's wrong with you? I can't do that. You can't do that."

"Please," Anthony said, "do what I asked. Go and get Melody." Then he sat down and undid his pink bowtie.

About the Author

Heather Caruso was born and raised in Sydney, Nova Scotia. As a young woman, she moved to the city of Toronto. It was there she met, and later married, her husband, Sal.

Now settled in Kelowna, British Columbia, Heather and Sal have a combined total of three sons, and six grandchildren. She wrote a children's book for them back in 2014 which sold out both of its printings.

Heather loves living in the Okanagan Valley and all the scenic views it provides her. She likes to spend her spare time with her sisters and writing stories.

In These Pages is her first collection of short stories which aims to capture the nature of everyday life.

About the Illustrator

Tao Caruso was born and raised in Kelowna, British Columbia. His creativity and drawing skills inspired his passion for the fine arts at a young age. Throughout his school years, he has picked up hobbies such as mountain biking and various other sports.

Tao attended the Centre for Arts and Technology in Kelowna, British Columbia, from 2014 to 2016. Today, he works as an animator for Yeti Farm Creative.

As an animator within the industry, Tao is particularly drawn to the ways he is able to incorporate his talent into the world of film and games. He aspires to create pieces of art with an aim to connecting communities together.

In These Pages

Manufactured by Amazon.ca
Bolton, ON

25247551R00079